The Royal Diaries

Jahanara

Princess of Princesses

BY KATHRYN LASKY

Scholastic Inc. New York

India,
1627

My father has four wives, but I am the daughter of the one he loves most, Arjumand Banu Begum. I, too, am a Begum, a princess. My name is Jahanara, daughter of Khurram, granddaughter of Emperor Jahangir, great-granddaughter of Akbar, the greatest Moghul ruler of India, and great-great-great-granddaughter of Babur.

I have diamonds the size of my small toe, and rubies the size of beetles, and I have thirty servants and eight elephants trained specially for me. I have everything except freedom. We are all of us imprisoned: my mother, my father, my younger brothers, and my younger sister. In tents hung with gold cloth, we drink from emerald-studded chalices and yet we are prisoners.

It is not our fate to be prisoners in a small princely kingdom controlled by a Rajput Hindu prince. It is our fate to rule an empire. My father should be emperor, Shah Jahan, Emperor of the World, and my mother should be

Empress Mumtaz Mahal, Jewel of the Palace, and I should be Begum Sahib, Princess of Princesses.

But we are not any of these because of The Snake. Yes, that is what I call her. She is the empress now but I call her The Snake. She is my grandmother but not my real one. She is my father's stepmother. I hate her. The world hates her, but they fear her and they call her Nur Mahal — Light of the Palace. But to me she is The Snake and she coils into my dreams at night. She strikes, hissing, into my thoughts. She poisons all around her, and, worst of all, she holds two of my brothers hostage. I have two more brothers — Prince Shuja, who is almost twelve, two years younger than myself, and Prince Murad, who is just three — and then there is Princess Raushanara, who is eleven.

Nur Mahal took Dara and Aurangzeb hostage three years ago. My father had been accused of rebelling against his father, Emperor Jahangir. But it really wasn't so. This was Nur Mahal spreading rumors against him. She hated my father and she wanted my grandfather to designate another heir to the throne — my father's brother Shahriyar. My grandfather's brains were addled by drink and opium. It was said that Nur Mahal secretly ground the opium into his food and constantly gave him the strong spirits, despite the warnings of doctors. In any case, she turned his mind against my father. Things came to a crisis and troops

were sent to march against my father. He was forced to make a bargain. The terms were that two strongholds under my father's command in the Deccan be given directly to his father's, the emperor, imperial guard. The second demand was that Dara, who was ten, and Aurangzeb, who was seven, be delivered to court as hostages. If this were done my father would be forgiven.

It is because of The Snake that I do not sleep and now feel ill. But I cannot tell my mother why. She has enough worries without my telling her The Snake dreams. But now she threatens to call the doctor since I look so ill.

December 2, 1627

This is my dream and I shall confide it here in this diary that my mother gave me. If I mark it down perhaps it will go away. But first, before I write down the dream, I must explain the truth behind this dream, the truth of my step-grandmother.

Nur Mahal was the daughter of a Persian nobleman and his wife. They had, however, become very poor and decided to travel to India in hopes of better prospects. It was on this journey that Nur Mahal was born. The journey was rough and there was hardly any food. They decided that there was

no way a baby could survive and that they themselves might have a chance if they abandoned the baby. So they did, alongside the road. Perhaps they were hoping that another, more prosperous traveler might find the baby and save it. But when they had traveled no more than an hour they became filled with guilt and turned back for the infant. The sun had risen high in the sky by this time, and they hastened, for they feared that the baby would die from the heat. There was no shade along the road. But when they drew near the spot where they had left the child, they saw a dark shadow rearing up and heard the happy coos and gurgles of a baby. Imagine their surprise, their horror, when they found the baby cool and happy under the protective shade of a hooded cobra, the deadliest snake in India.

That is a true story. Some say that the cobra nursed her by feeding her tiny drops of its venom and thus she was able to withstand any poison her enemies might devise. I am not sure if that part of the story is genuine — although it is true that many have tried to poison Nur Mahal and never succeeded.

So I dream of Dara, Dara with his dark and dreamy eyes. In my dream I see him sleeping. He is in a bed next to Aurangzeb, and I see a dark, almost liquid movement on the floor. I can hear my brothers breathing softly in their sleep. And beneath the sound of their breathing is the

whisper of a snake slithering across the floor. For some reason I know that it is going to my brother Dara's bed and not Aurangzeb's. It stops by Dara's hand, which hangs over the edge of the bed. It coils, rears its head, and spreads its hood. Just as it is about to strike, just as the forked tongue comes out, there is a deadly glint in the slitted eyes. I recognize that light. It is evil and the face is not that of a hooded cobra but of Nur Mahal — Nur Mahal, Light of the Palace. I always wake up just at that moment.

December 3, 1627

I dreamed The Snake dream again.

December 4, 1627

And again.

December 6, 1627

Sati-un Nissa, my mother's lady-in-waiting and our tutor, tells me that my studies are suffering. She presses me as to what is wrong. Although I love Satty she uses all her clever wheedling ways: the harem is talking, she says. Indira, my father's third wife, who is Hindu and a terrible gossip, is spreading rumors about me. "Who cares?" I say. "Indira is a gossiping old pig. Aba never visits her." Satty scolds me. How can a good Muslim girl even speak the word "pig"? Shame on me. I shrug. "Your mother will call the physicians," she says. "Pish," I reply. "You might be ill but you are still fresh," she adds, then taps the air lightly by my shoulder. For no one of a lower station is ever permitted to touch the body of a princess, not in affection or reprimand. Therefore, the air is kissed or tapped accordingly. Still it hurts. I respect Satty. Next to my mother, she is the most intelligent woman in the harem. I crave her approval.

Later

I think Satty might be right. The harem is gossiping. And it is not just Indira. Aba's first wife, The Persian, we call her, Tali, who is quiet as a mouse and hardly ever speaks, now tries to engage me in conversation. She has never paid a bit of attention to me. It is rumored that she once lost a baby girl who supposedly looked like me and that it is too painful for her to talk to or even come near me, but now she does. And Aba's fourth wife, Samina, who is as sour as lemons, suddenly gives me a smile every now and then.

But it is not just the words spoken. I see their looks. It is easy to read the faces of harem ladies. We, the ladies and girls of the harem, spend our lives behind lattice screens, the *jalis*. We are never to be seen by the world outside, nor heard. But through the openings that make the stone look like lace we can hear and we watch — always, we watch. In our silent lace cages in the *zenana*, the apartments of the harems, we begin to learn how to speak the language of silence, the wordless speech of gesture. Our eyes are as important as our tongues. It is through our eyes that communications transpire. There is a story that in the harem of my grandfather during a *durbar*, the public audience when people and officials bring their business to the emperor, a certain Englishman for the East India Company saw something sparkling even brighter than the diamonds the ladies wear behind the screen. They were the eyes of one of the "little wives," a concubine of my grandfather's. Every day this Englishman would come to court, and every day he would see those eyes watching him. He fell madly in love with the woman and a tryst was arranged. The two met and became lovers. But then they were discovered. The Englishman was sent back to England and the concubine — well, Nur Mahal saw to her end.

So today I see the harem's eyes as I walk by. They slide slowly. They sometimes glint. They mean me no harm. They love me, but they are desperately bored. They seize upon anything out of the ordinary, any shred of gossip or news like jackals on a bloody carcass. Over a month now we have been in the Deccan on our way back to Rajasthan, our homeland when we do not travel on a war campaign. It does not matter that our tents are as sumptuous as palaces. We are nomads. We are as addicted to movement as my grandfather was to his opium. We cannot move out into the world, but we can move through it and watch through the pierced screens of our *howdahs* atop the elephants. In the palaces in Agra or Fatehpur Sikri or in Kashmir we have more freedom. There are gardens we can walk through, pools to bathe in.

Later

I am afraid to go to sleep. I do not want to dream the dream again. Someone comes. I must stop writing.

December 7, 1627

Panipat came to me last night. He is the chief eunuch of the harem. As such he is allowed to enter any woman's chamber at anytime. He knows all of our secrets. Panipat is fat and his skin is as soft as a baby's, but he does have a beard. Not a thick one, but it hangs down from his chin like a long curl of white smoke. He is very old. He was a eunuch in the harem of my great-grandfather Akbar. I love him dearly. And he came to me in my most private hour last night. He saw that I was writing. He reminded me that Babur my great-great-great-grandfather kept a diary "to keep his mind orderly." "Yes," I replied, and then paused. "Your mind is not orderly, Begum Sahib?" I looked up at him. He calls me Princess of Princesses even though we are all prisoners and my father is not yet emperor. My eyes filled with tears. And the story of my dream spilled out with the tears that ran down my face. Panipat held his puffy hand just above mine as if to stroke it if permitted. "You must tell your mother. This dream is significant. She will call the astrologers. Your nightmare might in fact be the key to unlock our prison."

This I do not understand, but I shall do as Panipat says. He is wise. He has lived in two courts under two different emperors.

December 8, 1627

I feel great relief. My mother immediately called the astrologer and we went into the *Ghusl Khana,* the most private of all chambers in our tents, where I repeated the story from behind a screen. On the other side of the screen the astrologer Abul Fazi and my father sat. Abul had brought his star charts. They began to discuss an ecliptic event that is anticipated in the next few weeks when Scorpio and Libra will both be rising. I was dismissed. But I am happy. I think Panipat might be right. I have in my unknowing way perhaps delivered a key to unlock us from our prison. I think because my mother and father are so smart they will know how to use this key. I must think of a wonderful present for Panipat. An immense pearl, perhaps. But it must be flawed. Panipat loves jewels, beautiful, huge jewels, but, and this is odd, he does not like perfection. He always demands an imperfection in his jewels. Perhaps such jewels are like him — an imperfect man, but in my mind a perfect human being.

December 9, 1627

I did not dream last night! This was the first time in days.

This evening

It was bedtime and I was surprised when Jumpha, my first serving maid, announced that Panipat was here. He had come with an offer to read to me. Panipat with his silky, slightly high voice is my father's favorite reader at bedtime, but tonight Panipat said my father was not feeling well. He gave me a wink. I felt a thrill well up in me. The wheels of whatever plot my mother and father and the astrologer have devised begin to turn! I really know none of the details of this plot, but my mother has promised me that no matter what, I must not fear. All will come out well.

Panipat did not even ask what I wanted him to read. He had arrived with a book — the Babur-nama, my great-great-great-grandfather's autobiography pieced together from his diaries. He went behind the reader's screen near my bed. I heard him groan as he lowered himself onto the silk cushions. I even heard the air whistle softly from the cushion as he settled in. I was very alert because I felt there was purpose to Panipat's selection. I knew I would learn something of this plot that is afoot if I listened carefully to the passages that he chose to read to me. A bowl of rosewater with a candle floating in it was by my head. The scent of roses mingled with Panipat's lovely voice.

"These were my throneless times," he began to read. "My followers and I, now reduced to less than three hundred, used Khujand as a base for our night raids." I was not really familiar with this passage. It described the hard times when Babur had lost vast territories in Persia and places so distant from India as to be unimaginable. I might have found these passages boring before, if I had heard them, but now they had new meaning. Panipat was reading to me of the throneless times because that is precisely our situation. And I was to take courage as Babur had taken courage. "My men and I were starving. We were reduced to eating the flesh of dogs and chewing the leaves of trees that had dropped. . . . It passed through my mind that to wander from mountain to mountain, homeless and houseless, had nothing to recommend it."

I blinked at these words and then laughed. "Panipat," I asked, "how can he make a joke at such a time?"

"He was a brave man. Only the bravest can laugh when faced with disaster. And do you know the recipe for courage?" He did not wait for me to ask but answered, "One part wit, one part daring, and yes, one part fear. After all, there can be no courage if there is no fear."

December 10, 1627

I sit behind the screen in my father's sleeping chamber and write to distract myself. Panipat has told me that courage is one part fear, but where is my wit? Where is my daring? My father's condition grows worse. His skin looks like ashes. Envoys from the Rajput have arrived to tell us that a doctor will come soon. I sit behind the screen with my mother, Ami, as my father's chief minister talks in a hushed voice. He points to copper vessels that contain fluids from my father — his urine and phlegm. My father lies gasping on a pallet, fanned by two servants. Suddenly there is a terrible retching sound. An attendant lifts my father's shoulders up. A jet of red issues from his mouth. My mother screams.

Later

My father is dead. His body has been washed and set in the coffin. His three other wives are upset with my mother for not letting them visit him in his last hour. I am numb. I shall never forget the terrible scene of his death. The blood, so much blood. It was everywhere. Ami had flung herself across his body. She would not let anyone near.

Only Panipat and the chief minister were able to finally pry her off of him.

So now at last we are permitted to leave the Deccan. The stupid little Rajput prince no longer fears Nur Mahal's wrath, now that the true emperor is dead. Yes, he is allowed to leave in a coffin to be buried in his homeland near Agra, where he was born. Instead of a real emperor we have that insipid little Bulaki. That is his nickname. It means "nose ring," for he is so easily led around by Nur Mahal. He is what they call a Winter King, for winter is the shortest of seasons here. Nur Mahal really wants my uncle Shahriyar on the throne but he is sick. He has the rotting disease. His fingers are like stumps. His face looks like melted wax. And where his nose should be he has instead a small silver beak. And my handsome Aba, my father, lies dead in a coffin.

Soon it shall be my birthday. I shall turn fourteen. I care not a wit now. I would give up all my birthday celebrations in exchange for my father's life. To think that I used to count the days until my birthday. It seems so silly now.

We are to leave in the morning at first light, but only a small party of us. Much of the harem is to be left behind. It is bad enough thinking of my father dead, but nearly as bad is thinking of seeing The Snake again — Nur Mahal with her thin-lipped smile like a knife blade.

The glittering eyes. I am trying to have courage. I am trying, but where is the wit? Where in the world did Grandfather find the lightness to make a joke in his throneless times of danger?

January 1, 1628
Fatehpur Sikri, Rajasthan

We have traveled very fast and last night passed out of the Deccan. Now we approach Fatehpur Sikri, the city built by my great-grandfather Akbar.

We are near Agra, and for some reason my mother and the astrologers confer to decide which day is most propitious for our entry into Agra. I do not see what there is to discuss. We have lost all. With Aba dead why should it matter anymore? Why should anything matter? Who knows what Nur Mahal will do with us? My dear mother's father, my other grandfather, Asaf Khan, who happens to be Nur Mahal's brother but is as different from her as a monkey from a parrot, will come to greet us. I love my grandfather very much. At least I can look forward to seeing him.

January 2, 1628
Fatehpur Sikri

Today is my birthday. I had nearly forgotten it and now what I am about to write is unbelievable. My birthday wish has in fact come true. My hand trembles with joy and wonder. How can a world be turned inside out in the space of a few seconds? But here is what happened.

My grandfather Asaf Khan arrived and approached the bier of my father, which was set in the main courtyard of Fatehpur Sikri. He began the traditional obeisance for a dead emperor when suddenly the lid of the coffin opened and my father rose. Alive and healthy! The other wives swooned behind the screen, and I might have myself if Panipat had not come to my rescue. "Courage! Begum Sahib, courage!"

I turned to him and whispered, "Is this the wit part?"

He smiled broadly, and a huge guffaw tore from his flabby chest.

I shall write more later and explain this astounding event when I recover from my shock.

Later

Panipat has explained all. This must be the best-kept secret ever. The only people who knew that my father was not really dead were my mother, Panipat, Satty, the astrologer Abul Fazi, my father's imperial steward, Kareem Sind, and his most devoted general Khan Jahan Lodi. It seems that when I revealed my dream it was interpreted as a very bad omen. Abul Fazi felt that if we could escape in any way from the Deccan before the eclipse of Scorpio by Libra, perhaps certain courses could be avoided. I know that when Panipat spoke using words like "certain courses" and "events" and "configurations" he was really speaking of the harm, or perhaps even the deaths of my brothers held hostage, and naturally the loss of the throne for my father.

It was decided that the only way an escape could be achieved was if a trick was made of my father's death. Thus, he pretended illness and then — this is perhaps the most amazing part — on the morning that the envoys of the Rajput came, my father drank three entire goblets of goat's blood! It was goat's blood that he vomited, not his own. For the past two weeks as we traveled out of the Deccan only my mother, his imperial steward, and Panipat were allowed in the presence of the coffin, which traveled upon my father's favorite elephant, Banuri, in a howdah. My mother sat shrouded in the howdah and would open the lid of the coffin to let in sufficient air. She fed him as well, slipping in cool drinks and morsels of food. In the darkest parts of the night, Abul or Kareem Sind would mount the elephant and take care of my father's personal needs. And on these occasions my father would actually climb out of the coffin and stretch himself in the confines of the howdah. Thus he managed. And now we are here.

Asaf Khan has already sent his swiftest riders to protect my brothers. Nur Mahal is to be placed under guard. I asked Panipat when my brothers would come back to us. Again the astrologers must be consulted. At this moment Abul is working on his charts and with his astrolabe to fix a favorable date for our entry into Agra.

Tonight when Jumpha brought my nighttime cup of almond tea I saw her hesitate after she set it down as if she wanted to say something to me. So I said, "What is it, Jumpha?"

"I beg your pardon, Begum Sahib." I was startled that she was already addressing me as Princess of Princesses. "But I wish you to know that I am happy for you so much that your father is alive."

Her simple little speech touched me deeply. I know it takes great courage for a serving maid to address any of the royal family about anything but the most practical matters. Indeed this is a revelation to me. I never thought of servants thinking about anything but the most practical matters.

January 5, 1628

Here at Fatehpur Sikri we are not short on astrologers. There is an entire pavilion called the astrologers' pavilion where they meet to discuss the motions of the stars in the heavens and how they might determine the lives of people on Earth. I love this city. It is built entirely from dark pink sandstone. There are vast outdoor plazas, and when they pull the silver curtains in the archways, so no one can peek in, the females of the harem are permitted to go and entertain themselves. In one of these plazas is an immense Pachisi board and we play Pachisi, using our servant girls as tokens on the board.

January 6, 1628

Now everyone is exchanging places with their servant girls to be tokens on the Pachisi board. My sister,

Raushanara, was immediately discovered, of course, because she is still such a child and very short.

These days here at Fatehpur Sikri feel like a time of enchantment. We now know that Aba shall be emperor and Ami shall be his empress. There is a lightness to his walk. All these years Aba has fought for my grandfather Jahangir and defended his territories. Every one of us children, except for myself, was born on the war campaign trail. But my father has always said that he is no warrior, although he seems to do it well. He says instead that he is a builder. He is devoted to beauty.

Akbar, too, loved beauty and made many nice palaces for his wives, for indeed he had three hundred!

January 7, 1628

It has all been decided — the dates by the astrologers, that is. We shall depart tomorrow for Agra at one minute after three in the morning just as Venus is rising, so that we might arrive in the city on the twenty-eighth day of this month. We shall stop on the way at the tomb of Akbar to pay homage and then proceed. But once we arrive at Agra we must wait according to the astrologer's proscriptions for twelve days for my father's coronation. That will be

February 9. And the twenty-sixth day in February is the day that the astrologers have decided will be the most propitious for the return of my dear brothers.

These instructions all sound rather complicated to me. Satty just laughs and says, "You think it will be simple when you get twelve astrologers together?" She is right. They have been jabbering away night and day in the astrologers' pavilion. Each one thinks he has the more precise interpretations of the heavens.

I must go. The *muezzin* calls for noonday prayer. What do I pray for in my secret heart of hearts as I bend toward Mecca? My brothers, and their safe return, naturally. I would pray for a husband, but that is impossible. You see, many Moghul princesses are never allowed to marry. Had my father not been emperor I could have married. But I think this is the price I must pay. And I do it with pride, for I know Aba will make the greatest emperor of India since Akbar.

January 8, 1628

Venus has risen and through the gold mesh curtains of the howdah I smell the scent of mangoes. My father's elephant Banuri is near to ours. Mangoes are Aba's favorite fruit. He has arranged for scores of mango trees to be delivered in the next convoy from the Deccan, where they grow thickly in some places.

Raushanara and Satty and I share the same howdah atop Tambur, named for Tamerlane, the first Moghul to successfully invade India. His true name was Timur-i-Leng or Timur the Lame. And my dear Tambur is himself slightly lame. But he has been a steadfast elephant. Very smart and a hard worker. Now they give him only the lightest loads — me, Raushanara, and Satty, who is very skinny. They are both asleep. I do not know how they can sleep. I am too excited.

This is the beginning of our coronation march. This is the first time in a long time we have marched not to war but to celebration. And now we travel in true imperial style, for we are not pretending to mourn. The elephants have been painted with colorful designs. Flowers burst across Tambur's trunk and face in saffron and turquoise. The *mahouts*, the elephant drivers, were up all night painting them. In my father's court a mahout must be not only a reader of the elephant's very intelligent mind but an artist as well.

The canopies of our howdahs are no longer white, the color of mourning, but cloth of silver. The screens of gold mesh are often strung with diamonds for catching the moonlight. Sometimes, like now, as Satty sleeps, I part the screens and look at the moon with my bare eyes. It's quite thrilling.

January 26, 1628
Sikandra

We have been in Sikandra now for several days, visiting the tomb of Akbar. Tonight it is the wives' and children's turn to sit within the mausoleum of the great emperor and offer flowers and prayerful thoughts. We are carried there on our palanquins.

The walls are painted with Christian scenes as well as Hindu ones. Akbar was known for his tolerance of all religions. One of his wives was an Armenian Christian and many were Hindus. He allowed them all to practice their rites within the harem. Now, here is a secret that I know but no one else does, except a very few. Panipat told me this because he knows that I can keep a secret. Akbar is not really buried on the third floor where we pray. His actual body and that of his first wife are in the crypt beneath the first floor. This was done to fool grave robbers!

January 27, 1628
Six miles from Agra, along the Jumna River

Today we move on to Agra. We shall arrive at the gates two minutes after the stroke of midnight and then wait for twelve days. The throngs on the road are immense. A guard must ride ahead, clearing the people, and there are all sorts of people. We pass by peasants and Rajput chiefs. They are all joyous at the sight of my father. I see through my screen a woman pounding a meager handful of rice in a pit to make it explode and fill the cooking pot more generously. Beside her I see a rich man in his cart with a pair of white oxen, their horns sheathed in copper. I see boats on the river. Our royal couriers are steady and run alongside to clear the way, with a whip in hand and little bells that jingle fixed to their turbans, announcing our arrival.

It is so exciting as we gain our first glimpse of the Red Fort. I see the massive sandstone battlements glowing in the moonlight. A thousand or more torchbearers are stationed atop the walls. It has been more than a year since we have been to the Red Fort. My father is already talking about changes for it. Jahangir let it fall into disrepair. But it is not only that Father wants more gardens, more pools, and fountains. He has other plans as well. Indeed as soon as the bright *shamiana* tents are pitched, I have been told to expect a visit from Aba. He has matters to discuss with me. Aba often uses me to listen to his notions about gardens and the design of buildings.

Later

Aba did come to speak with Mother and me. Under his arm were scrolls and scrolls of his favorite architect's drawings, his plans for the palace of the Red Fort. My quarters shall be added on to and redone. I worry that Raushanara might become jealous. He tells me not to worry. But how can I not? What he plans is so splendid. It is as if Aba is creating for me a little palace within a palace. They have already begun to sheathe the roofs in copper, and he described an immense marble, water-filled basin with a design of large lotuses carved into the bottom. He said that the walls in many places in the palace have deteriorated badly and he wants to make the walls of my little palace exemplary. Therefore he brought out a paper with a grid and some colored paints. I am to design the way I would like the jewel inlay to look.

Aba then took out another piece of paper and handed me a pen. "You must make a list of the gems you want to use. Of course for the deepest red — that reddish brown —

it will be jasper. The best comes from Cambay, I think."
So I began writing the list:

Carnelian — Baghdad
Quartz, jade amethyst — the Nile
Emeralds, rubies — Ceylon

Aba sighed and I looked up from my writing. "Why do you sigh?"

"I am thinking, you are but fourteen years old and you write such a lovely hand and you read so widely. I hear from Satty that you have plunged into the Hindu epic the *Ramayana*."

"Oh yes, Aba. It is wonderful."

"But to think." My father paused. "Akbar could not even read this himself."

"What do you mean?" I was puzzled.

"You did not know, child," my mother interjected, "that Akbar was illiterate?"

No, of course I never knew. No one had ever told me. All I had ever heard was how brilliant Akbar was. How could he be so brilliant without knowing how to read? Ami replied mysteriously, "Because he was so brilliant! That's the point."

I must say, this last evening on the eve of entering Agra was the most pleasant. It was just the three of us. In the smallest chamber of the large tent I painted, Aba even sung. A servant brought in the *thali*, an immense plate with several little containers of food, and we just leaned against our pillows and picked what we wanted. There were lentils and tandoor-baked chicken, as well as pigeon baked in a similar manner, and many vegetables, muskmelons, and raisins from Persia. And of course mangoes, Aba's favorite. He ate so many that Ami cautioned him, but he just took an extra piece of *paan*. The paan leaves are filled with betel nuts and other condiments and they aid in digestion. Or so they say. They never helped me.

But it was such a perfect evening. It was like a dream . . . just Aba and Ami and me.

P.S. Did I mention that a new diary has begun to be kept? Not for me, but for Aba, to record his reign as emperor. Abdul-Hamid Lahawri, one of the most learned gentlemen in my father's court, has already begun writing down everything. And many imperial artists have been assigned to make beautiful paintings of the important moments. When I sit behind the screens and observe my father's receptions and audiences, I now see this man constantly not far from Aba's side, writing, writing, writing.

January 29, 1628

But now a bad dream. The Snake again. Why should I dream of that piece of evil now? She can no longer harm anyone I care about. But her slitted eyes come to me in the dark of my sleep. I do not dream the whole dream as I used to. Indeed it is just she, Nur Mahal, who comes. Sometimes it is just the slither that I hear. Last night I awoke screaming and Panipat had to come in to soothe me. I dreamed I felt her shadow suddenly slide over my face — the shadow of the cobra's hood. It was terrible. I made Panipat sleep right next to my pallet for the rest of the night. I wish I could have reached out and held his hand, his nice, soft puffy hand, but I cannot touch him, nor can he touch me. It is sometimes a very cold and lonely place in which I live.

January 30, 1628

Disturbing rumors fly about. It has been said that Bulaki, the Winter King, and Shahriyar, the prince with the rotting disease, have been murdered. Well, some say murdered, some say put to death. Ordinarily I think death is death. But if one is put to death it suggests that some authority has commanded it. And indeed they are saying that it is my father. I cannot believe my father would do this! I cannot believe he would kill anyone anyplace but on the battlefield.

How can a man who just the other evening sat with me and my mother and talked of art and architecture, as Aba did, order the death of others?

February 1, 1628

I know why I dream this dream. It is because in exactly three days when we enter Agra we shall see Nur Mahal once more. I dread it. She should be honored, for my father will agree to meet her.

February 4, 1628
At the gates of Agra

We passed through the immense gates of Agra. I had forgotten how big they were. A silence fell over the crowd as our elephants passed. It was very strange. I do not think I have ever heard silence in India. At the main gate with the drawbridge there is a bazaar. Raushanara and I were feverish to look out, to part the mesh screen, but I felt Satty's eyes drilling into my back. Allah knows what she would do if we did something so crude. All she did last night was lecture us on our new positions — how we must remove ourselves even further from the public. "How can we do that?" I asked. She looked at me knowingly. Yes, she guessed that in the past we have peeked. But the bazaar was so interesting. I saw jugglers and dancers strung with tinsel. But most of all I really want to see my father atop his elephant in a cloak of gold with pearls, his broad chest festooned with jewels and on his head a white turban. Right in the center of his turban is the Ruby of Lahore, the city where my father was born. Such a ruby has never been seen. It is almost a third the size of a man's fist. Even from here all closed up in this stupid howdah I can see glints of its red light spangling the street, the people.

February 8, 1628

Tonight I can hardly sleep, for tomorrow my father shall be crowned Emperor of India. It is too bad that the building of his throne, the one that he is calling the Peacock Throne, cannot be completed in time. In fact it will take seven years, but no matter. There will be magnificence enough.

Later

I have at last thought of the perfect gift for Panipat. The imperfect pearl. It is stitched onto the decorative work of my *kameez*. The pearl is brown with a white streak. A slight flaw is a harbinger of good luck. Indeed the Koran tells us that it is a sacrilege to aspire to perfection, for it is an insult to Allah.

Later
The Palace of the Red Fort, Agra

I think my Aba is too particular. The palace is not nearly as shabby as he led us to believe, and the zenana is in nearly perfect condition, not to mention my little palace within the zenana. Oh, how I do love it. I have wonderful views, and the day before our arrival, the stoneworkers and plumbers had just finished the marble basin in which I can bathe. When I arrive it is filled with water, and roses float on top. In every single niche, of which there are at least twenty, vials of perfume have been placed, which release their fragrance. And should I want to bathe by candlelight, little floating dishes each bearing a candle are placed in the water. This is exactly what I will do. For by the time we arrive it is nearly dark and Satty is talking away about all the things we must do before the coronation. There are jewelers to be met with, and cosmetic artists, and the seamstresses, and our own ceremonies in the zenana must be planned to celebrate our new emperor. But I am tired. I say anyone who wants to see me must see me in my little palace. And if I am bathing, so be it.

So be it: I float in my pool among the roses that brush my toes, and the water dances with the reflections from the candles. Indeed from the high archways where the light comes in there is even a splash of moonlight on my scented bathing water.

Jumpha kneels by the poolside with a plate of figs and slices of mangoes, which she feeds me as I float by. The dust of the roads dissolves. The closeness of the howdah evaporates. The rocking gait of my elephant is a dim memory. Now I float in this marble pool in a bower carved from stone. This is what I am doing when I hear Panipat enter:

"Nur Mahal has arrived! Your presence is required at once."

Later

She was not supposed to have come until tomorrow. And first she was to attend the morning durbar, the general audience, and then have the smaller audience with Aba. But this, Ami tells me, is classic Nur Mahal: her strategy is surprise, to throw the opponent off balance. Well, that she did. Ami and I sat behind the lattice screens in the *Machli Bhawan,* or Fish House, as it is sometimes called for reasons I do not know. It is actually a sunken courtyard with screened pavilions on all sides for the harem. Ami is gripping my hand so tightly it nearly hurts. I want to say to her, "You are empress, or shall be tomorrow; this woman cannot hurt you." It is as if my mother and I can speak without words. I know her thoughts as we sit there: a snake can hurt anyone. What does a snake know about an empress or the poorest woman beating rice?

I press my face closer to the screen. Nur Mahal stands very straight. I can see from the set of her jaw that she is angry. I know why. She wanted to be received in the most secret of council rooms, the Ghusl Khana, where no eyes would be watching her, but now there are hundreds. The other three wives sit with us and my sisters and little brothers; then the little wives sit behind all the other screens, plus the eunuchs, the servants, and the scribes. No one would miss this. It was genius of my Aba to meet her here. He has thrown <u>her</u> off balance!

Again I press my face closer to the screen. I feel my mother gently tug me back. I hear my father in an unusually loud voice give the customary greeting to Nur Mahal. Except now there is one difference: he addresses her as Empress Dowager. "I would have of course preferred to meet in the Ghusl Khana but when you arrive at the last minute like this certain plans cannot be changed. My vizier and chief minister are doing business with the gentlemen from the East India Company."

What was left unsaid was the most important of all: you are no longer of any significance. King Charles of England and our trade with the British are infinitely more important to our future than you. You can stand there in your diamonds and your fine silks but what the English want are the very fabrics that you scorn as being peasant cloth — our ginghams and our calicoes, our muslins and dungarees, our taffetas and alliballies, our humhums and jamdannies — dyed with colors that can be found only in India, woven to perfection.

And, he might have added, I shall not ignore these good men who were so rudely overlooked by you.

Nur Mahal stood very still for long minutes. She

betrayed no fear, no anger. And then she spoke three words: Mountain of Light.

There was a huge collective gasp from all the women of the harem. She turned her head slowly toward the screens and smiled her narrow, bladelike smile. Her eyes glittered. She wanted the unthinkable. She wanted the Koh-i-Nor diamond!

She was of course dismissed without explanation. My father would not dignify the request with an answer. I must speak with Panipat tonight when I plan to give him his pearl and ask how she could have even thought of this.

Later

"She wants it to curse it!" Panipat said simply as he turned the flawed brown pearl over in his hand, clearly relishing its luster and the odd tricks the light played upon it because of the white, cometlike streak. Curse it? I was confused. Then he explained that Nur Mahal knows she could not rightfully have it or keep it forever. But if she could get it into her hands for a brief time, she and her *fakirs,* the mendicant Muslim wonder-workers, could perhaps cast a spell, and in that sense she would possess the diamond and those who possessed it. "But," I argued, "would that not be against the Koran?" Panipat laughed deeply at this. The multiple folds of his belly shivered up and down. "Since when," he said, "has Nur Mahal ever followed the Koran? She manipulates it to suit her needs. Her teachers, the *mullahs*, the muezzins, all serve her before they serve Allah."

Panipat also told me that Nur Mahal might not be gone for good. That my father is too kind and that there are rumors that he will make a place for her in the palace, within the zenana but far from us. He might build a special apartment for her. "Why? Why must my father be so kind?" I asked Panipat. And Panipat said it is not completely kindness. "Your father would prefer to have Nur Mahal close where he can watch her than far away where he does not know what evil she is stirring up. She is a devil, this woman."

February 9, 1628

In all the mosques of the city a prayer has been read this morning in the name of Shah Jahan and his Empress Mumtaz Mahal, Jewel of the Palace. An hour before, my Aba was Prince Khurram and my mother Arjumand Banu Begum. And I? I am now Begum Sahib Jahanara,

Princess of Princesses. And even if more princesses are born to my dear mother only I shall be Princess of Princesses. I take extra care with my dressing this day.

I am wearing the most elegant *churidaars* made especially for this day. The pants are of silver cloth and as all churidaars, are very tight from the ankle to the knee. The ankles, though, are trimmed with yellow diamonds and emeralds that have been sewn on to look like daffodils. Daffodils are my most favorite flower. The tunic robe is a *pairhan* of a semitransparent material with silver gilt braid and red-and-green tinfoil designs depicting iridescent beetles' wings. Underneath I wear a close-fitting bodice in the Hindu style — a *cholis.* I shall wear my emerald ankle bracelets and two toe rings, both diamonds that Ami gave me. Jumpha helps me with all this and is most particular. She even takes a soft cloth to all the foil embroidery to give it extra shine.

While my father is crowned in the *Diwan-i-Am,* the Hall of Public Audience, we ladies of the court await him in the zenana. But we can hear now the rolling booms from the drum house where the kettledrums of gladness and rejoicing are beat. This signals that my father is now emperor and has received the Timurid crown first worn by his ancestor Timur-i-Leng.

He has promised to come directly to us as soon as the

official ceremonies are over. We have woven garlands of jasmine, marigolds, and roses to put around his neck. And Mother has had court musicians compose a special piece. I am so excited I cannot write anymore. I shall finish reporting on this day, if I am not too tired, when all is done.

Later

The emperor arrived with a parasol held over his head with golden fringes that looked like rays of the sun. He now wore the raiment of a king, a magnificent *jama*. The robe was embroidered with yellow and white diamonds. His velvet curl-toed slippers were stitched with diamonds on a background of rose velvet. I had to blink, for although I could see that he was my father, my Aba, he was more.

We brought our gifts for the new emperor but there were rewards for us as well. Two eunuchs followed Father in with a small chest. I wondered why it took two to carry such a small chest, and then the emperor commanded them to place it at my mother's feet and to open it. The gold in that chest lit up the room. There were 200,000 pieces of gold and 600,000 rupees, and he whispered to my mother that she will receive an allowance of another million rupees a year. An emperor's gift to his beloved empress. Then another chest was brought in for me. It took only one eunuch to carry it, but my father made a great ceremony of it and insisted on opening it himself. Then my father explained that the gold pieces in the chest amounted to 75,000 and the rupees numbered 400,000, with 600,000 more for an allowance. As he whispered he slipped something from his cummerbund and put it in my hand. "I shall explain later," he said. For my sister and each of my brothers and Aba's three other wives there also received chests filled with rupees and gold. Nearly all the ladies of the court received some handsome reward.

Our celebration feast was most memorable. After months in the Deccan it is so good to have a full kitchen again with nearly three hundred cooks. Close to five hundred dishes were prepared. Needless to say <u>all</u> of my favorite foods were included. I could, of course, have eaten only *julabmost*. To my mind the best of these fruit ices is the lemon mixed with rosewater. The chefs then sprinkle rose petals over the top. It is such a special treat after the Deccan, where the chefs could not get ice from the mountains to make it and the saltpeter used to cool the water in which the ices were kept was limited. But there were many other fine dishes. There were *Nimki* pastries. Murad, who is just three, must have eaten his weight in Nimkis. There was pomegranate soup as well. Chicken was served a dozen different ways, and lamb perhaps two dozen ways. It was so wonderful. The chicken had been cooked with poppy seeds and cashews and was served on a bed of minced lamb. There were no beef dishes out of respect for Indira and the other Hindu women of the court, because Hindus never eat beef, of course. But Indira alone must have had three helpings of the chicken and lamb dish.

It was a glorious feast and the high steward and his assistants walked in, each bearing silver and gold and china and copper platters that were tied up in beautiful silk cloths. When they untied each dish the food was so pleasing to the eye with the garnishes of rose petals and sometimes leaves made of silver and gold that one might have thought it was a display of the emperor's jewels. Soon the air swirled with the scent of cinnamon and cardamom and all the spices both sweet and pungent.

Now that Aba is emperor, however, all the food must be tasted first in case of poisoning. This makes everything long in coming and Murad began to whine. But it was worth the wait. We ate in the garden under a shamiana. The canopy was made of sheer gold cloth through which we could see the stars. Despite the heat of the day it felt cool, for this garden ripples with water. Water sprays from fountains and courses down wall niches. Aba and Ami and my brothers and sister and I sat on a raised marbled platform in the middle of a pool, which we reached by stepping-stones. The mists of the fountain kept us cool all evening.

While we ate there were music and dancing girls. They danced my favorite *kathak* dances from the north. Each dancer wears *ghungroos,* the rows of bells on her ankles, and as she moves, the bells jingle according to a musical pattern composed for the dance. It is all dependent on the footwork. There is one dancer, Madha is her name, who has such skillful footwork that she can jingle just one bell at a time!

February 10, 1628

I nearly forgot to write about the small package that Aba slipped into my hand on his return from the coronation. When I opened it I found an exquisite miniature of a woman like no other woman I have ever seen. Aba told me that two days ago when his vizier met with the gentlemen of the East India Company, many gifts were presented. He selected this one, a miniature of their most beloved queen, Elizabeth I, who died not so many years before I was born. This woman captivates me. Her skin is quite white and her hair a brilliant red. Her face is narrow and comes to a near point at the chin and she has an enormously high forehead. She is not pretty but very, very . . . I search for a word . . . compelling! And there is an intelligence in her eyes that almost crackles. They called her the Virgin Queen, for she never married. And when I asked Aba if this was unusual, he said, "Yes, in England they have different customs, and princesses are allowed to marry." So I look at her and I wonder why she chose not to and then I realized. She is a queen! There is no king. She has everything. She is in a sense both queen and king. If the Moghul court permitted women to rule would I sacrifice that chance of truly ruling, of being both empress and emperor, to marry? I am not so sure. This is a pendant miniature, so I might wear it around my neck as well as hang it in my bedchamber near my bed where it is now. I look at her in the yellow glow of my oil lamps as my reader reads to me an ancient Persian poem. Her hair seems almost in flames in this light and her eyes are steady. This woman gives me courage — for what, I am not sure, but she gives me courage.

February 12, 1628

In exactly two weeks our brothers shall be returned to us. We are all so excited. I have made a calendar to mark off the

days and Raushanara, Murad, and Shuja are excited as well.
I plan to let each of them take turns marking off the days.
We cannot imagine what our brothers will look like now.
They have been gone so long. Shuja wonders if Aurangzeb
will have a beard. I tell him that is ridiculous. He is only ten
years old. Shuja is obsessed with the notion of whiskers. He
checks his face constantly for any sign. Aba has a most noble beard. It connects to his sidelocks with beautiful curves.
His barber is excellent. Satty proposes that we all make pictures of what we expect our brothers to look like and then
give the drawings to them when they come. I think it is a
wonderful idea, if we have the time. There are so many coronation activities, elephant fights, and banquets, there is
hardly time for anything. We haven't had lessons for days!

February 14, 1628

Twelve days until our brothers arrive. But, and this is the
bad news, Nur Mahal will stay in the palace. My father has
already arranged special apartments for her. He promises
us that we shall not have to dine with her, or even see her
that much. She is old and much weakened, he says. But I
can tell by the look in my mother's eyes and in Indira's
that they do not believe it.

Later

Nur Mahal is kept or perhaps chooses to keep a distance from us. But even at a distance she can be frightening.

February 15, 1628

Our lessons have resumed. Satty now has it in her head that I must not only learn I do not know how many *suras* from the Koran, but be able to recite them perfectly. All this in a mid- to high Persian accent, an accent that will "melt a mullah's heart!" Satty is so dramatic! She closes her eyes, tips her head toward heaven, and presses her clasped hands to her breast. I did an imitation of her for Ami the other night. Then of course Ami begged me to do my other imitations. This is apparently my hidden talent. It must remain hidden because too many of the ladies of the harem would be very angry. I am especially good at imitating walks. When I do Samina, Ami turns red with laughter. Samina walks like a chicken on *bhang*. She flaps her elbows like wings and her head bobbles back and forth. And then there is Indira, who walks like one of the cows sacred to her religion. The Hindus worship cows. So in any Hindu village we pass through, one might see cows simply untethered and walking about, sticking their noses into anyone's business — be it a merchant selling rice or a baby making pee pee by the road. Nobody says no to a cow. They are harmless. They sway their heads in gentle curiosity and that is exactly how Indira walks, ambling along and swaying her head.

Usually, of course, I have imitated women, for it is women that I mostly see close up. But I am working on a few men. You see, when they have important dinners in the great hall of dining, the women of the harem may observe from a screened gallery above. And I have picked out a very peculiar fellow from the East India Company. He must be seen to be believed, but even from on high I can tell that he is almost a perfect sphere. He is like a ball and his legs bow. Not only that, he bounces! The ladies of the harem call him Lord Bouncey Bounce. He bounces when he walks. And when he talks and even when he sits at the table he seems to bounce. I wonder if he bounces in his sleep.

February 18, 1628

Eight more days until our brothers come. The lessons are getting ridiculous. I mean, Satty is just piling on the work.

Shuja and Raushanara and I are now required to learn a long list of herbs and what ailments they remedy. I say, "For goodness sake, Satty, we are not training to be healers. Why is this necessary?" And she replies, "Are you never going to get sick in this life? Don't you want to know what the doctor is giving you and why? You want to let quacks treat you? Fine, go ahead, be ignorant, die."

So sweet, my Satty! But I do love her.

Later

> Borage for stomach disorder
> Valerian for headaches and calming of nerves
> Rose hips to cleanse urine

This is very monotonous. Raushanara and Shuja and I question one another, for tomorrow Satty will test us. I write truthfully that if it were not for Elizabeth — yes, that Elizabeth, the queen of England — I would not be studying so hard. I keep her miniature hanging before me as I study. It is said, so my father reports, that she was one of the most intelligent monarchs ever to rule. She has even been compared to Akbar! I can see that intelligence in her eyes. It inspires me.

February 23, 1628

Only three more days until our brothers come. The light of happiness seems to spill from Ami's eyes as she anticipates it. Tonight she and I talked long, just the two of us, imagining how Dara and Aurangzeb might have changed. I showed her my drawings and she said she dared not even picture them. She told me tales of when she was a girl growing up and how dear her brothers were to her, and then for the first time ever she told me how she and Aba met. It was at the Mina bazaar, which next year I shall be old enough to attend. The Mina bazaar was started by Great-Grandfather Akbar. It is an imitation market. Vending stalls are set up filled with cheap trinkets, and on this one day of the year women of the harem are permitted to come out from behind the screens of purity, although they are heavily veiled, and pretend to be vendors of goods and haggle just like the common women in real marketplaces.

Ami was standing in the same stall as her aunt the Empress Nur Mahal. It was the first time she had been brought to court. She was just my age and wore her hair in a single long plait that had been twined with lilies. There were gloves in her stall and many young men had come up, but she had been too shy to speak or even meet their gaze. But Aba broke the silence. He said, "Oh, that I were one of those gloves to fit upon your hand." She said she blushed furiously and Nur Mahal kept poking her in the ribs and finally hissed, "Speak! Speak! The prince thinks you are dumb."

And Aba said, "She speaks with her eyes, Your Highness. For even behind the veil I can see them and I know what they say."

And what they said was love. But they had to wait a few years before they were married. By the end of the story Ami and I were both crying and then I had a thought. "Did he buy the gloves?" I asked. Ami thought this was the funniest thing she had ever heard. She laughed so hard she rolled backward off her pillow and nearly turned a back somersault. I love my Ami's laugh. She is so gentle and so demure, but when she laughs it comes from so deep that it rumbles, almost like a man.

February 24, 1628

Two more days! Today we leave for Fatehpur Sikri, for that is where we shall be reunited with my brothers. I think last night was a night I will long remember for sheer happiness — the anticipation of my brothers' return, the closeness with Ami, the stories, and the laughter. Do you know that the only lines in Ami's face, although she is almost thirty-five years old, are the ones that come from laughter?

March 5, 1628
Agra Palace

I know that it is odd I have not written these days. After all the time anticipating my brothers' arrival I write nothing. I cannot explain it. I know the others feel the same thing, perhaps not as sharply as I do, but no one wants to speak of it. There has been a change. Not with Dara but with Aurangzeb. I shall describe the moment of reunion as best I can.

We awaited my brothers in the *Diwan-i-Khas,* the Hall of Private Audience. This hall has a unique design. The room has a very high ceiling, and within it is a central pillar, the top of which is a circular platform. This is joined to balconies along the walls by four bridges. The emperor sits on the platform and those in attendance can approach him by these bridges. On this day of February 26, my mother, the empress, shared the platform with the emperor. It was said to be the first time an empress had ever shared the platform since it had been built. Together they waited for my brothers to be brought across the bridge by my grandfather

Asaf Khan. I waited in a gallery with my other brothers and sister. I actually saw their shadows first, for it was morning and through an eastern-facing window a slant of strong, late winter sun flared. Their shadows seemed indistinguishable perhaps to most, but for those of us who have spent so long watching from behind screens, the slightest trace of a difference can be detected. And I noticed that one shadow seemed to glide effortlessly forward while the other seemed to hesitate. I watched my mother. Even from a distance I could detect her trembling, and a pulse seemed to leap in her neck — very tiny pulsing but I could see it. Then I saw Dara. He could not restrain himself a moment longer and came rushing over to embrace my parents, his wide-cut boy's coat flaring out behind him. But Aurangzeb seemed to continue at his own slow, stilted pace. Had he been injured? I wondered. But no. He approached and then bowed stiffly to my mother and father. Greetings were exchanged.

I would think no more about it. Our own meeting with our brothers was to come in a few minutes when Raushanara, Murad toddling and led by his nurse, Shuja, and I would cross the bridge. From my first step I saw Aurangzeb's eyes fasten on me in a most piercing stare. He stood perfectly still, and I began to think this would be the longest short walk I had ever taken, but then once more Dara could not contain himself and flew out over the bridge to scoop us into his arms. He had grown a great deal and was at twelve a good head taller than Aurangzeb, who is two years younger. But Aurangzeb had the eyes of an old man, no longer a child. Aba, of course, whooped and laughed at our boisterous reunion on the bridge but I could see a shadow briefly flicker in Ami's eyes. Did she notice the same things I did?

We stood on the platform for some time and Aurangzeb did greet me, but his eyes seemed to focus on the miniature that rested in the hollow of my neck. We then adjourned to the Jodh Bai Palace, which is part of the *panch mahal*. We went there through the secret passage, which on this occasion had been perfumed and laid with the richest carpets. We sat down to a sumptuous meal. But all through the meal Aurangzeb stared at my miniature. It made me very self-conscious and I kept touching my throat. Dara, however, was chattering away, asking me what I had been doing. What was I reading, harem gossip, and so on.

I could not imagine what was happening until three days later when we had returned here to Agra and all of us children were in what is sometimes called the Garden of Golden Scattering because of all the orange and yellow flowers. There is a family of peacocks that lives in this garden and they are quite tame. The father peacock came up to me in the path and spread its immense and dazzling tail. Aurangzeb snickered. I turned to him and asked what was so funny. He looked at me and said softly, "Perhaps he shares your vanity, sister."

I was perplexed. "What vanity?" I asked.

"The vanity of a human who wears the image of another around her neck."

"Why is this vanity?" I asked. "Why is wearing this image a vanity and these rubies on my wrist not, nor the pearls around my ankles?" I was not trying to be argumentative. I was genuinely curious.

"It is vain," he replied. "Any human likeness is an affront to Allah."

"But Aurangzeb," I protested, "it is only in the mosque that such decoration is forbidden."

"And should your body not also be a mosque, a temple to Allah and as sacred?" He stared hard at me, a stabbing light coming from his little old-man eyes.

But then Dara came to the rescue. "I overheard you, brother. So am I to understand that you believe this peacock here with the design of eyes in his tail feathers is also a disobedient Muslim?" I began to giggle nervously.

Aurangzeb stalked off and I was left speechless.

Dara whispered to me that he would come and explain some of the changes in Aurangzeb, but then that day he had to leave with Father and Aurangzeb and Shuja to go on a special hunt. They return this evening. But I must say that I have been so sad. I need to talk to Dara and I can see the concern in my mother's eyes as well. Aurangzeb has changed.

March 6, 1628

The weather turns very hot. In another few weeks we shall leave for the north, for Kashmir and Srinagar and the hill country where the cool winds blow down from the mountains. It won't be too soon. I cannot concentrate on my studies between the heat and the worry about Aurangzeb's odd behavior. I wish it were just me he was so strange with, but it is with Ami and Satty and everyone. I noticed as soon as he got here that he was always praying and constantly reading the Koran, copying out long passages, muttering them as he walked in the garden. And his disdain for the court painters is so obvious that I fear it will provoke Aba.

I had a very strange thought after the incident in the garden. I remembered how Panipat told me that Nur Mahal wanted the Koh-i-Nor diamond so she could place a curse on it and thus possess it and all those who possessed it. I wondered in the darkest moment of the night if indeed Nur Mahal did not in some way cast a spell upon my brother Aurangzeb.

No matter, I shall continue to wear my pendant with the miniature of Queen Elizabeth. I shall not be scared by my brother's ridiculous notions of what is religious and what isn't.

March 8, 1628

Dara tried to explain to me about Aurangzeb. He says it is no curse set by Nur Mahal. It is simply his way. He said that when they were first given over as hostages, Aurangzeb was so full of grief and longing that Dara thought he might simply die, die of a broken heart. He said I should remember that Aurangzeb was barely eight at the time. Somehow Aurangzeb got a notion that this was some sort of punishment. Dara said that nothing he could say could convince Aurangzeb that it was not. He said Nur Mahal was merciless in her teasing of him, calling him crybaby and worse, for he had begun to wet his bed. And then he began to pray a lot. He felt Allah would somehow lead him to an answer. "His faith deepened as his heart broke," Dara said. "And then he stopped crying and he seemed better. He was better. It was as if his heart had mended."

But I wonder, how can a broken heart mend in such a brittle way?

March 9, 1628

Aurangzeb is frustrating Satty as well. He refuses to study certain subjects because he thinks they are "impure." So he sits and knits prayer caps while we read poetry. He finds particularly offensive our reading of the Puranas, the ancient myths of the Hindus. Satty reminds him that our grandfather had a Hindu mother and he just sneers. Then Dara reminds him that our great-grandfather Akbar counseled that we should learn about all religions and study the art and literature of all people. And Aurangzeb says quietly, "I disagree." We are all terribly shocked. This is almost like a desecration. Satty is so stunned that she closes her book.

It is odd but with Aurangzeb's contempt for all things Hindu, indeed all things that are not Muslim, I find myself drawn closer to Indira, Aba's Hindu wife. She is very learned. And I feel sorry for her because Aurangzeb has been very rude to her.

Later

So rude that Ami has just scolded Aurangzeb! Our mother says that if Aurangzeb does not improve his behavior she will take it up with Aba. I must go off to a nighttime polo game.

March 10, 1628

Aurangzeb is slightly improved. The polo game was wonderful. Dara got to play! He handled his pony well although he never did connect with the ball. Nighttime polo is beautiful. It is played with a luminescent ball of *pala* wood. They set the ball into a fire until it just begins to smolder and then it starts to throw off an eerie light. It was a beautiful evening, and we sat atop our elephants and watched from our howdahs. We drank pomegranate juice and snacked on sticky sweet buns. Between periods of the game, the musicians played. Aurangzeb knitted prayer caps through the entire game. We could tell that Aba was irritated. He wanted Aurangzeb to observe so that he will learn about polo. Indira knows much about the game, as it is a Hindu sport and her father was a champion player. I really am liking her so much more.

Tomorrow begins the Persian New Year celebration, *Nawroz*. It coincides with the solar birthday of my father. There shall be a weighing of the emperor, as such is the custom. He is weighed twice a year on his birthday, according to both the solar and the lunar calendar. Beggars are sought out as well as favored noblemen and an amount equal to his weight is distributed in gold, silver, and grain.

March 11, 1628

Aba sits like a golden sun in the pans of the scales as they weigh him. I watch through the screens of the largest garden of the fort. Hundreds of people await my father. The beggars are put toward the front. On the counterbalancing pan I believe a bag of wheat flour is placed. Another one is needed and yet another before the scales are balanced. There is a cheer from the beggars, as this flour shall be distributed to them. Next come bags of precious cloth, followed by other foodstuffs. All this will go to the poor as well.

But now the excitement mounts as a bag requiring four servants is placed on the scales. Aah! It is too heavy. A sigh passes through the crowd like a light breeze. A secretary to my father comes out. He carries a small silver shovel and opens the bag. One, two, three, four shovelsful of silver and jewels are taken from the bag. Finally the scales balance. A cheer goes up. The precious gifts in this bag shall be distributed among my father's nobles. A special portion is allotted for General Khan Jahan Lodi.

Now the *nautch* dancers begin to dance. The music is infectious. Off to one side I see the court painter Bhola with his cups of ink and paints and sketch tools, and of course Abdul-Hamid Lahawri sits and records each weighing of goods.

March 13, 1628

Everyone is very busy as the court prepares to move to Kashmir. It cannot be too soon. The heat is terrible. This is how bad it is: Panipat, for our amusement, got an egg from the kitchens and cracked it on the marble of the zenana terrace. In no time at all the egg began to sizzle and then the clear part turned white. Murad, who is just three, thought this was an absolute delight. He looked up at Panipat as if he had performed a miracle. For the rest of the afternoon he kept nagging for Panipat to do it again.

But then his nursemaid promised to take him to see the elephants after his nap. Murad loves to visit the elephants, and he is a favorite among the mahouts who tend them. There is one in particular that has taken quite a fancy to Murad. It is a grand old female named Gulnar. She wraps her trunk around him and nuzzles him gently. He always brings her betel leaves, which she loves. So with that promised visit we have hushed the child.

May 1, 1628
The palace at Srinagar, Kashmir

I know it has been long since I have written, but the journey from Agra to here takes such a long time. And much of the time I did not feel like writing. I was very worried about Ami, for she did not seem herself and was exceedingly tired. But now I can report a happy reason for that. She expects a child come November. I do hope she keeps this one, for she has lost the last two babies. She is ever so much better since we have arrived here, however.

The cool breezes that blow down from the mountains are just the tonic for her. Everything is so green. I am always amazed by the greenness when we return to Srinagar. Aba calls Kashmir the jewel of northern India. I myself like to think of the bordering mountains with their snow peaks as the crown, the glades and surrounding crystalline lakes as a multicolored jeweled necklace, and the beautiful garden of Farah-Baksh as the most precious jewel in the necklace. The name of the gardens means One Who Bestows Joy in Persian. We spend our entire summer here in the pavilions of this garden. And it is always a most joyous summer.

We have our studies in the garden, and this place is so beautiful that even the lessons do not feel like lessons. We are surrounded by carpets of brightest flowers, purple drifts of evening stock, and little white snowdrops. But I believe that my favorite living things in these gardens are not the flowers but the Chenar trees. Standing eighty feet tall, they are like old friends, steadfast and always here. It is against the law to cut a Chenar, for we consider them sacred. And I believe they are. Dara believes a Chenar tree has a soul.

He wrote a beautiful poem in honor of one that we often sit under. I shall copy it out here.

Old friend,
Your ancient spirit stands guard
Ever patient
Ever watchful
A sentry in an unseen world
A friend to all in this one

I love my brother Dara.

May 3, 1628

Dara and I had a long and interesting discussion. He was telling me about the Hindu belief in reincarnation. Reincarnation means souls can live multiple lives, because they are reborn after death into new "vessels," he calls them. So one could be reborn a beggar or perhaps a chicken or an emperor. I have heard of this doctrine, of course. But Dara in his deep mysticism thinks about everything in new and strange ways. He looked toward the sky, sparkling now with constellations, and told me we cannot even imagine the vastness of the heavens. He thinks indeed there could be other worlds. Nor can we imagine, he said, the vastness of time. Dara believes there is more time than the sages and all the mathematicians could ever account for. I said, "You mean more than thousands of years?" He nodded solemnly.

"More than millions?" I asked.

He nodded again and said, "Perhaps billions, sister." The notion is both frightening and fascinating. In such a limitless universe where do we figure, even though we are prince and princess and children of the Emperor of the World?

May 5, 1628

Dara has commenced a large project. He is much taken with the Hindu religious epic of the *Bhagavad Gita*. We have been reading portions of it in Hindustani with Indira. He has decided to attempt to translate these portions into Persian. Dara feels that there are similarities between our Islamic faith and that of the Hindus. His notions intrigue Aba. And I think Ami is very proud, for here is a son who thinks in the tradition of Akbar, who was a unifier of beliefs. But Aurangzeb is outraged. He threatens to go to the mullahs and report what he calls Dara's "desertion of the true faith."

Aurangzeb's narrow beliefs lead to nothing as far as I can see except praying and knitting prayer caps. But what does he pray for?

Later

What does Aurangzeb do? Well, here is one thing that is shocking. I saw him talking in a shadowy corner of the garden this evening with someone. A woman. I stopped behind a Chenar tree and stood perfectly still. When the woman turned I saw it was Nur Mahal. Now, why would

Aurangzeb be speaking with Nur Mahal, the woman who teased him so torturously that he began to wet his bed? Nur Mahal was his jailer! This is most perplexing.

May 12, 1628

A special picnic was planned for today. There are two islands in the middle of Lake Dal here in Srinagar. One is called the Silver Island and the other the Gold. We cross the lake on the slender boats called *shikara* to the Silver Island, also called Char Chenar for the four Chenar trees on each corner. It is our favorite place to go. In the middle of the island is a pavilion built by my grandfather, and there are gardens bursting with roses and marigolds and all sorts of vines.

I simply love our picnics here.

As we were reclining on the carpets, eating the last of the mangoes, Shuja suddenly said, "Didi," for that is our nickname for Indira, "tell us a Krishna story." And then Murad, who had almost been asleep, suddenly sat straight up. "A Krishna story," he begged. "Krishna! Krishna!" he began chanting. Dara and I and others joined in the chant.

We love Indira's Krishna stories about the naughty blue Hindu god. They are very funny and so engaging. I did notice, however, that Aurangzeb was sneering throughout and he kept whispering to Raushanara. Ami gave him a sharp look, for it is rude to talk while someone is trying to tell a story. When Indira finished, we all applauded and called for another Krishna story. So she said, "I shall tell you another and this story is really true." She took a deep breath and another sip of wine, and settled her large, fleshy body into the silk cushions. She was wearing a bright pink kameez, and I thought she looked like the big pink clouds that collect over the mountains. She wears a red spot in the middle of her forehead, as do many Hindu women, and a bright little diamond pierces the right side of her nose. Ami says I can have a nose piercing on my next birthday.

When Indira finished her true story a deep silence settled upon us. But then Aurangzeb made a rude noise and Raushanara began to giggle ferociously. Ami looked daggers at them both. I have never seen such a fierce look on Ami's face. "You are excused from this gathering!" she hissed. "The two of you. Sadia!" she called Murad's nursemaid. "Take these two infants and deliver them to the boatman to take back to the palace immediately."

This was the supreme insult. For a ten-year-old and an almost twelve-year-old girl to be escorted from a gathering by the nursemaid of a baby was shameful enough.

Both Aurangzeb's and Raushanara's faces turned dark red with embarrassment. They had been publicly disgraced in the most severe manner. But I was frightened. There was a look of absolute hatred in Aurangzeb's eyes. I felt no good might come of this.

Indira, though, was wonderful. She looked about with a bright smile, as if she had some delicious secret she was hiding, and said, "Do you children know that on this very island there is a statue of Krishna? Yes, your grandfather Jahangir had it made and placed there in honor of his own mother, Jodh Bai, who loved the Krishna stories."

We were amazed and asked that she lead us to it. Then it was Dara's idea that we make a *puja*. So we followed Indira through a winding path edged with snowdrops and violets to a deep glade, and in the thick of a drift of ferns we spotted the bright blue statue of Krishna. We each brought with us an offering — a lotus flower, a handful of coconut bits, a sweet, some banana. For my puja I brought a small bouquet of violets and a piece of my favorite almond candy.

It was a perfect day! And I cannot believe that I once thought Indira a fat old gossip. I think of her now as a large, warm comfortable woman of elegant learning. Have I grown up, or is it that Indira has become more likable?

May 14, 1628

I cannot believe it. Indira is desperately ill. Wazir Khan, the royal physician, has been with her all night. She became ill at dinner. It was very embarrassing, for her stomach was seized in a terrible tumult and she was sick all over herself.

At first Wazir Khan thought it was poisoning. But thank heavens he now thinks it's nothing more than an overdose of betel nuts. But the odd thing is, Indira does not like betel nuts, so we cannot figure out why she would eat them. It is always difficult when the doctor comes to the zenana. He cannot directly see the sick woman. He must put his hands through openings in the curtains that surround her bed and perhaps knead her stomach, or take the pulse in her wrist. But then another woman must stick her head in and describe how the sick person's tongue appears. Is it coated or not? If her eyes are clear, are the pupils small or dilated? Indira's were said to look like pinpricks. The doctor was given the pans of her body's wastes, and he will examine these very closely in his laboratory.

May 15, 1628

Indira is much better this morning. I went to sit by her bed and read to her. Ami came with me and held her hand.

Later

We have had shocking news. Wazir Khan has reported from examining Indira's vomit that the betel nuts had been pulverized to a degree that is suspicious, for indeed they had not been digested. Thus, logically, if not digested, they should have been in larger, more fibrous fragments. At first I did not understand the looks of astonishment on both Ami's and Aba's faces. But then it dawned on me. Someone must have ground the nuts into a powder and put them into her food or drink. Who would do such a thing?

May 16, 1628

The mystery is solved. Aurangzeb and Raushanara are the culprits. Raushanara broke down and came crying to Ami. But this is even more shocking: Aurangzeb says he did it as his Muslim duty, because "she befouls Allah with her Hindu gibberish." I thought Aba was going to strike him right there. But he is wise, my Aba. He left, his face white and rigid, and went immediately to speak with a royal mullah of the court, Mustafa Azir. Aurangzeb was called into the meeting with Aba and the mullah. It is said that Aurangzeb entered the Diwan-i-Khas looking quite smug. He must have thought the mullah would vindicate him. But quite the opposite. Mustafa Azir said Aurangzeb had brought shame to his religion. That he uses it as a cudgel. That he had violated the very tenets of Islam. And he was reported to say, "What good is it that you pray five times a day, if you are vicious to your father's wife? Your prayers count for nothing."

Aba has ordered five stripes be laid upon Aurangzeb's back. And Raushanara is ordered not to leave her quarters until Ramadan begins, which is in another week.

But I am disturbed by something. I remember now that it was the night before the picnic that I saw Aurangzeb and Nur Mahal speaking together. Could Nur Mahal have something to do with this? But why would she want to hurt Indira? Indira is no threat to her. I was not going to tell anyone about seeing them together. But now I think I shall tell Dara.

Later

I have told Dara. Dara disagrees that Nur Mahal is part of this mischief. He says we must not look to place blame. Some people simply are the way they are and Aurangzeb is one. Dara and I discuss this punishment of Aurangzeb's and conclude that he shall never again be tempted to hurt Indira or any other of Aba's wives or little wives in such a way. But as we have said, he will not forget it. And this in itself might not prove well. Aurangzeb is a vicious person. He was first humiliated by our mother at the picnic and it led to this. Now he has been humiliated by our father and the chief mullah. What will that lead to?

May 17, 1628

Ramadan begins tomorrow. We must not eat or drink all day, from sunrise to sunset. It is a bit difficult. The days seem long. No picnics, of course — at least not during the day.

May 21, 1628

This is so boring. I really hate Ramadan. I know I shouldn't say it, but I do. Aurangzeb loves it, of course.

Later

Fourth day of Ramadan. This is so boring. Twenty-six days to go.

May 25, 1628

All I do all day long is think of food. Today I spent the entire morning dreaming of julabmost and *balashahi* pastries. Balushahi are my favorite pastries. They are fried in oil and then dipped in syrup and sprinkled with crumbly nuts.

May 26, 1628

Today Dara and I made lists of our favorite food.
    Here's mine:

    Orange julabmost with rose petals and mint leaves
    Lemon julabmost with chopped apricots
    Apricot julabmost with sugared mint leaves and grapes
    Lamb kebabs with scorched apricots
    Halwa, a sweetmeat with almond paste
    Barfi, another sweetmeat

Gulab jamun, soft round balls flavored with syrup and rosewater

It is so odd, though. I dream all day of delicious foods, but come evening when we eat, it seems all I am really hungry for is *raita,* the yogurt with cucumbers that is nothing special.

Dara says we are shrinking our stomachs.

I said to Dara, "Is that so good? After all, Allah made our stomachs so they could hold food to nourish our bodies and we could praise Allah."

June 1, 1628

Satty is always mad at us for not attending to our studies. She caught me making another food list today when I was supposed to be learning a poem in Persian. "All you think about is your stomach," she screeched. "I give you the finest example of Persian poetry, the music of the heavens, words as bright as the Koh-i-Nor diamond, and you think about your silly stomach and julabmost, silly girl!" Then she batted the air near my shoulder in reprimand. Aurangzeb smirked.

June 4, 1628

I am tempted to write this in the smallest letters, for this is very secret. Dara and I have done something very bad, but maybe it is not that bad. You see, Dara said he thought about what I had said — how Allah had made our stomach to nourish our bodies and praise him. Then he thought about what Satty had said when she scolded me. He put them together and decided we should try to sneak some food. Why should we not be able to praise Allah or listen to the music of the heavens? Why must we starve ourselves in order to praise Allah and find true enlightenment? We cannot even concentrate on our studies because of our thoughts of sweetmeats. Is this reverence?

So we eat. Dara is close to one of the eunuchs who is close to one of the cooks. He sneaks us little dishes of sweetmeats and when he is able, cups of julabmost.

We are both doing ever so much better in our studies and there is less than two weeks left of Ramadan.

June 10, 1628

I saw something very disturbing in the harem garden today. There was a bent old man with his hand rake, but he was not a eunuch. I could tell immediately and I could not understand why such a man would be admitted to work in the gardens of the zenana. Aurangzeb was nearby and so I asked who the man was. He said that his name was Hamid and that he had once served in the court of our grandfather as a councilor. I was shocked. Why is he here now on his knees in the garden? "Look closely at him," Aurangzeb said in a strange voice. So I did, although I was some distance, and I noticed that there was something odd about his eyes.

"What is wrong with his eyes?" I asked.

"He was a spy," Aurangzeb replied, "and his punishment was to have his eyes stitched shut. That is why he can work in the zenana gardens. He can see nothing but he seems to be able to rake despite his blindness."

I gasped at the horror. I know the punishments are harsh in the court of the Moghul emperors. It is part of our history. Men are executed often in a grotesque manner. A thief might have his hand cut off. A man who covets a woman of the harem might be killed by being crushed by an elephant. Elephant crushing is a favored method of execution. But somehow this shocked me the most.

Later

I am very worried. I have a strange sense that Aurangzeb knows somehow that Dara and I are receiving food from the royal kitchens.

June 11, 1628

I must find Dara. I don't know where he is this morning. But I am frightened. Right before I was to meet with Satty to practice this week's suras from the Koran I was sitting in the garden, and again I found myself staring at the poor blind gardener. I was not aware that Aurangzeb had come up behind me. He whispered softly in my ear. "Yes, it is quite sad, is it not? And do you know what the punishment is for a treacherous cook?" My blood ran cold. "His tongue is cut out."

I began to tremble. But I would not give Aurangzeb any satisfaction by asking why he would say such a thing. I simply got up and walked away. My brother is cursed. I believe this. But cursed or not, Dara and I must stop eating. No one must be mutilated because of our transgressions. My hunger is treacherous if I must satisfy it in such a way.

Later

I found Dara and he agrees with me. We must stop sneaking food. There is only a little less than a week left of Ramadan, in any case.

June 18, 1628

Last night we had the end of the Ramadan celebration. It was a most wonderful feast — hundreds upon hundreds of dishes. The cooks have invented a new dish in honor of Aba. It is called *Shahajahani biryani*. It is a rice dish, which I believe has everything in it from the empire. There are almonds, and apricots and ginger and layers of lamb, and chicken and threads of saffron, which make it a beautiful orange color. It was so delicious. And I ate five different kinds of julabmost. It all tasted so good. I am glad Dara and I stopped our foolish practice of sneaking food. To think that someone could have been horribly punished because of our greed.

June 24, 1628

A niece of Indira is to be married. Aba wants her to have a very fine wedding. I think this is a way of honoring Indira. Aba has been especially attentive to her since the horrible trick that Aurangzeb and Raushanara played on her, and so has Ami. I think they want her to feel loved and valued. It can be difficult for her, being the only Hindu wife of Aba's four. Samina is downright nasty to her, and Tali, The Persian, does whatever Samina tells her to do, so she more or less ignores Indira. The wedding is to be in October after we return to Agra. It will be a Hindu wedding with Hindu dancers brought from all over, and Hindu priests. Hindu weddings to my mind are much more fun than Muslim ones. I am going to ask Ami if I can have my nose pierced even though it will not be my birthday yet.

I still see the blind gardener often and cannot help but think about his horrendous punishment. I know that my Aba, because he is emperor, would perhaps do the same thing if a spy were caught in his court, and yet I try to imagine that he would not. I mean, Aba is so kind, so thoughtful. He goes out of his way. For example, this wedding for Indira's niece. I wish I could stop thinking about this.

June 30, 1628

Ami has lost her baby! This is the third baby she has lost in two years. We are all so sad. I was hoping she would have another little girl. Raushanara does not even feel like a sister to me anymore. She is so thick with Aurangzeb and she also grows close to Samina. I really do not know how she can stand Samina.

July 1, 1628

Raushanara has a new jewel. I do not know how she got it. It seems to be somewhat of a mystery. It is a ruby and she wears it as a pendant hanging from her neck. The first time she wore it she fondled it very obviously and looked directly at the miniature of Queen Elizabeth that I wear around my neck. And then when Samina complimented her on it she said, "Yes, jewels are vastly superior to the wearing of an ugly white woman's face, and I do not offend Allah with my decor."

I smell a rat here.

July 3, 1628

The rat is Nur Mahal. She gave the jewel to Raushanara. Why, I wonder. I am very nervous about this. First I see Aurangzeb talking with Nur Mahal and now this. And Dara believed I was too suspicious when I thought Nur Mahal had something to do with Indira's sickness. I am going to speak to Panipat about this. I certainly cannot disturb Ami. She is still unwell.

July 5, 1628

Panipat, too, is worried. I should have spoken to him when I first saw Aurangzeb with Nur Mahal in the garden. He said Nur Mahal has invited Aurangzeb and Raushanara <u>and</u> Samina for tea in her apartments twice! He said he must think what to do next. I asked him why does he not tell Aba right away, and he said that one must work very carefully around Nur Mahal. Her thirst for vengeance is unquenchable and when she strikes she strikes quickly like a cobra.

July 10, 1628

Ami is still very weak. The doctor comes every day. I spend many hours reading to her, as she prefers my voice to that of her usual reader. I can tell Aba is worried. He usually goes on a hunt after Ramadan but it was canceled this year.

July 20, 1628

Ami is much better. She was able to accompany us on a picnic to Silver Island on Lake Dal. Once more we went and saw our old friend Krishna and made puja offerings. Aurangzeb and Raushanara did not go, of course. I could tell that Raushanara really wanted to go. But she is under Aurangzeb's power. She does everything he tells her to.

July 21, 1628

I have not been feeling well at all. This frightens me, for it was when we last went to Silver Island that Indira became ill. Supposing someone has tried to poison me? Someone like Nur Mahal. My stomach is in knots.

August 5, 1628

I have been very, very sick these last two weeks. My mother now reads to me. It was not poisoning but an illness that affects my urine. Luckily one of the things that Wazir Khan orders that I drink a lot of is something I love: pomegranate juice. But I hate the doctor's visits. It scares me to see his hands come through the curtains. They are thin and very white and have long hairs on the knuckles. He prods my belly and my back. And then his voice hisses at me, "Relax, Begum Sahib! Relax! I must feel your stomach!" How can I relax with these disconnected hairy-knuckled hands coming through the curtain? I imagine them attached to a most horrible monster on the other side. This is just awful. I wish there were women doctors. It would make everything so much easier. Satty sits inside the curtain with me and describes my tongue and how my eyes look and the color of my skin.

I must remain very still all day long. Rest is the only cure for my illness. I am very tired all the time. I am so tired that I am not even bored. Writing this has taken all my strength.

Jumpha my servant is most solicitous and sings to me in the lonely small hours of the night. She has a lovely voice.

August 7, 1628

Ami is with me day and night. She tells me stories of when she was a girl. I always ask for the story of how she and Aba met at the bazaar. She told me something new this time — that the Mina bazaar was often called the Flirting Bazaar. But I do not know what the word "flirting" means. She tried to explain. It has something to do with playing and something to do with love. But I cannot understand it. She said it is like when a girl perhaps "makes eyes" at a boy. But I do not understand what "makes eyes" means. She said, "Oh, you know, you might look at a boy and then turn your head quickly away, but a playful light comes into your eyes." I said, "Ami, how can I understand this? I live with women and girls. The only men I see are the eunuchs or my brothers." Ami sighed. Ami didn't grow up in a harem because even though her family was noble, they did not live in the court of the emperor. She saw more than just brothers and eunuchs.

When Ami grows too tired, Indira comes and reads to me. I asked Indira about flirting. She was no more helpful than Ami. I asked her if her niece flirted with the young man she is to marry. She said she imagines she did. I feel as if this flirting thing is like a secret that everyone knows except me.

I told Indira I hope I grow well by the time of the wedding. She said of course I will.

August 9, 1628

I feel a little better today. Ami says I can have my nose pierced for the wedding even though it is not my birthday time yet. This is the only advantage of being sick. People are extra nice to you.

August 12, 1628

Aba came to visit me today and put in my hand a lovely, tiny diamond. "It is for your nose, Janni," he said softly. I am excited now. I must be getting better. I think having a diamond in my nose might make it easier to flirt. Because if it is as Ami suggested — the way a girl tosses her head and slides her eyes about with a dancing light in them — well, a diamond might add to this — a perfect little diamond flickering on the side of my nostril. But <u>who</u> am I going to flirt with? That is the question. The choices are less than inspiring. My brothers? Panipat, an ancient eunuch? A blind gardener?

Also I am sick to death of pomegranate juice. I care not if I ever see another pomegranate in my life!

August 13, 1628

Today I got up for the first time in weeks. My legs are so weak. A servant girl Chitra is allowed to touch me, for she has very strong hands. She comes to massage my legs and bend them. I am to press hard against her hands with my feet. This is supposed to strengthen the muscles.

August 16, 1628

Every day I walk a little farther. Today I went into the garden. I prayed that I would not see the blind gardener.

August 21, 1628

I feel so much better. I cannot believe how quickly I am becoming strong. Ami warns me not to do too much.

Jumpha was serving me my almond tea this evening and all of a sudden I saw her eyes begin to fill. "What is it, Jumpha?" I asked.

She set down the tea and tears began streaming down her face. "Begum Sahib, I am most thankful that you are well. I was so fearful." And then she fell to her knees and kissed my feet!

This simple girl amazes me. Her feelings run so deep. Why does she love me so? We have no bond. I only tell her what to bring me and when, fetch this, fetch that, take this message or that. It is an odd thought to me that a servant should have such feelings.

August 24, 1628

So much fun today. Cloth merchants came to present silks for the wedding clothes. Indira had the servant girls spread the cloth. She immediately eliminated some — "This one, the weave is uneven . . . this one, the gold thread is inferior . . . this design . . . is vulgar . . ."

September 1, 1628

Every day it seems that there are some preparations for the wedding. We must pick our clothing for this festivity or that, for the wedding celebration will go on for almost two weeks. Nautch dancers are brought to us and we decide which ones will be best for which events. I can tell that Samina is resenting all the attention Indira is receiving. It worries me. I think she is a very treacherous woman. I do not trust her.

September 2, 1628

I think Ami is noticing Samina's behavior as well. She is going out of her way to be nice to her.

Later

I think Ami spoke to Aba about Samina, for I see that Aba sat next to Samina tonight at our evening meal and invited her to keep him company afterward. He hardly ever does that. Samina departed the table gloating.

September 5, 1628

Allah have mercy! Now that mousy wife, Tali, The Persian, is whining constantly and looking about as perky as wet tea leaves. She is obviously upset that Aba is paying attention to Samina and not to her. It was fine when they were both left out but now he chooses to attend to one and not the other. Oh dear, it is all so complicated. Things would be a lot simpler if Aba had only one wife — Ami, the one he truly loves.

September 10, 1628

We leave for Agra in two days. We had our last picnic at Silver Island. We said good-bye to the peacocks in the zenana gardens. It is sad, leaving this beautiful place. I picked some petals from my favorite flowers. I shall stitch them into a small silk pouch and put them under my pillow to remember the scents of this, the most beautiful garden on Earth, Farah-Baksh, One Who Bestows Joy. I have known many feelings here in this garden. Joy is but one of them, but there have been sadness and fear and yes, confusion. I still do not understand flirting and this leaves a small hollowness in me that feels like sorrow more than ignorance. And I shall never forget the blind gardener, although I have not seen him since I was sick.

October 1, 1628
The Palace of the Red Fort, Agra

Everything in Rajasthan is so green. Indeed the green surprises me the way it did when we first arrived in Kashmir. Ami calls it monsoon magic. For indeed it does seem a miracle wrought by a fakir that a land that we left sere and brown and dusty can now be so green from the heavy rains that drenched it in our absence.

The palace, too, seems much transformed. Aba's architects and builders have been working night and day since we left. There are new apartments, new gardens, new pools and fountains, and the walls in the old rooms have been refurbished. Ceilings have been painted until they sparkle like jewels, and indeed the walls have been inlaid with new precious stones. My own apartments, which I thought could not be made any prettier than they already were, now shimmer with newly inlaid jasper and lapis lazuli. My favorite flowers and vines from the gardens outside have been brought inside and re-created in the most splendid gemstones. At night when my oil lamps are lit the flowers seem to shimmer, as if illuminated in some eternal springtime, on my walls. So even when their blossoms fade in the depths of winter, within my apartments it shall be spring and summer.

And tomorrow I will have my nose pierced. I am so excited. Indira will hold my right hand and Ami my left. Indira assures me it does not hurt a bit. She will mark the spot for the needle with a carmine dot. She says the hole must be placed just right — not too close to the crease of what she calls the nostril flap or the jewel will be "compromised." I have no idea what she means by this. Perhaps it will not show up well enough.

October 2, 1628

It is done. I thought it would hurt a teeny tiny bit. I was very grateful that both Indira and Ami were there to hold my hands — except that I was really the one to grab theirs. I became aware of how different their hands are. Indira's is large and chubby and Ami's is thin and bony. I was worried that I would crush every bone in Ami's hand when Sulochana, the nose piercer, worked. The worst part was not when the needle went in but when Sulochana twisted in the diamond. The diamond is on a spiral of gold and it seemed to take forever to turn it in. But it will never come out. Never.

There was very little blood. Just a speck. Ami says that this part of the nose has almost no blood. And my diamond looks so beautiful. I just love it. I keep running to my mirrors. And now there are tiny mirrored pieces embedded in the walls of my apartments between the gemstones. They are only for decorative purposes. But I catch the flash of my nose as I walk by, and it is as if the air is spangled with the light of the little diamond chip embedded in the flesh. Indira would allow Aba to give me only a very small diamond. She says it is "coarse" to wear a larger one like "Madame Pooja." Madame Pooja is one of the little wives. But she is not so little, nor is her diamond. She has very chubby nose flaps, and the diamond sets atop them like a big fat boulder. Indira is very funny about Madame Pooja. "I tell you, Missy" — Indira has taken to calling me Missy. We think it is an English expression that she heard someplace before she was in purdah in my father's court. "I tell you, Missy," she said, "I must squint my eyes closed when she comes near. And on a hot day when her face is all shiny with perspiration, well, it is just too much. Yes, indeed I should cast on a dark veil to save my poor eyes." Ami laughed so much she almost tipped over while drinking her tea.

October 25, 1628

This is the first time I have had a minute to write in almost a month. Shocking, yes! But explainable. Indira's niece Swarup's wedding has taken up all our time. The festivities — and such festivities: dancing, parties, pageants, and plays — went on every single night for two weeks. No wonder we are so exhausted.

I think my most favorite party was the henna party the day before the wedding. Three chambers in the zenana were set aside for the occasion and the best henna painters in the kingdom came to paint our feet and hands with intricate designs. All day long we drank juices and tea and nibbled sweets. Betel leaves spread with lime juice and spices were passed as we reclined against bolsters with our feet and hands propped up as at least thirty expert henna painters worked on us. Indira did not eat any of the betel leaves, of course, but the rest of us ate many and felt pleasantly tingly. Flute players serenaded and nautch girls danced. They had brought some special dancers from Madras who knew the classic forms of the *Bharata Natayam* dances. I was astounded to find out that in these dances there are twenty-two poses for the head and neck alone that an accomplished dancer must learn. While our feet dried some of us attempted the head poses. There are even certain ways of lifting and opening an eye! And hundreds of *mudras,* or hand poses.

Swarup, the bride, was giddy with excitement, and because she is very ticklish she turned even giddier as they painted her feet. We all began laughing and two eunuchs had to hold her while Bhagmati, the best of the painters, worked as quickly as possible on her feet.

I would not trade a minute of it. It seems as if every occasion called for the flinging of colorful powders. Throwing bright powder is a Hindu custom especially indulged in at any celebration of Krishna — except then they often mix it with cow's urine. Why, only this morning I combed the last of the bright pink from my hair.

The wedding ceremony itself of Swarup and Ravi seemed small and rather quiet compared with all the rest. A wedding camp was just outside the palace with scores of colorful tents for all the relatives. The ceremony was held in the garden where the *mandap,* a canopy, had been erected. The bride and the groom were led to the mandap. There are many interesting steps in a Hindu wedding. Perhaps the loveliest part of the ceremony is when the bride's parents perform the ritual of washing the bride's and groom's feet in coconut milk and water to purify them for their new life. And then the marriage vows are exchanged. The last part is so romantic: a length of white cloth joins the bride and groom and they walk around each other four times, signifying the four stages of life — childhood, youth, middle age, and old age.

We saw all this from behind the jalis. But there was a moment when the sun flared through the lacy openings in the stone screens, catching the colors of Swarup's bright costume, and the very air around us seemed to dance with streaks of red and gold. It was as if we were caught in some gilded moment.

But as beautiful as this was and as cheerful as the festivities have been there were, of course, moments of tension. Tonight, two days after all the ceremonies have concluded, there is another. It has just been revealed that Aba has bestowed on Swarup one of Akbar's emeralds as his wedding gift. My great-grandfather was famous for his love of emeralds and his collections are renowned. But so far Aba has given away only two of the emeralds: one to my mother and one to Indira on the occasions of their marriage to my father. This is yet another source to fuel the discontent of Samina and Tali—and, of course, Aurangzeb. Aurangzeb could barely conceal his disgust with what he called the "pagan obscenities" of this wedding.

I think it is so good of my father to do this, but I must admit I worry. Yet I am proud of my father. He truly is in the tradition of his grandfather Akbar. And although my

Aba's name, Shah Jahan, means Emperor of the World, and my grandfather was called World Seizer, I would think Aba might be called World Embracer. I have in my mind an odd image of my father. I see his arms as immensely, ridiculously long — so long that they can wrap around the world. And he wraps that world in a glittering embrace of true understanding, of love, of acceptance. So I think that the giving of the emerald to Swarup is most fitting. I do, however, have one selfish thought about the emerald: I wonder if I, who shall never marry, will someday, in some way, be worthy of the gift of one of Akbar's emeralds?

November 15, 1628

The days fly by now. The weather turns cooler. The flowers in the garden fade and drop their petals. It is hard to believe that a year ago we were prisoners in the Deccan. So much has happened since then. I shall turn fifteen in less than six weeks. But I shall never have a birthday to compare to last year when Aba rose from the dead!

Aurangzeb is not feeling well. His eyes are glassy and his cheeks are aflame with fever. I know this is perhaps not right to say, but I like him better when he is sick. I almost feel sorry for him. He looks a little bit frightened, more like the child he was when he left instead of that hardened man he has become. I wonder if perhaps I might go and try to make friends with him again. I want to be his sister. I want to be a true sister.

November 16, 1628

I set off this morning with the best intentions. I brought the Koran, and a servant followed me with a pot of Aurangzeb's favorite rose tea and a small tray of sweetmeats. I was determined to try. But then Raushanara slid out from his chambers just as I was announced. "He does not want to see you," she said quickly.

But I was not so sure. I had hardly been announced. There was not time for him to respond.

"Are you sure?" I asked.

"Yes," she replied.

Well, I was simply not willing to accept no for an answer. For the first time ever I asserted my authority as Begum Sahib, Princess of Princesses. And that is exactly what I said. "I am Begum Sahib, Princess of Princesses, and I command you to step aside. I shall hear directly from my brother whether or not he wants to see me, and I shall abide by his wishes."

Raushanara was stunned, but then quickly her eyes hardened into dark, little stones. For a split second she looked exactly like Nur Mahal. It made my blood run cold. But she did step aside. I entered and Aurangzeb actually seemed happy to see me. I read to him. He drank tea and ate a sweetmeat. He was very happy for the sweetmeat. He says they have given him nothing but nursery food — soft, mushy broths with no taste — for days. He asked me to come back tomorrow. I shall!

November 23, 1628

I have gone every day to read to Aurangzeb. All he wants to hear is the Koran. He knows it perfectly. It is hard to believe. If I make the slightest mistake in reading he corrects me. I was astounded the first time this happened. I asked how he had such a perfect knowledge. And he said, as if this were nothing, "Oh, I am not perfect yet, but soon, I hope. I have memorized almost three-quarters of the book."

It is quite boring to have such an unvaried diet of reading. But if that is what he wants and if that is what brings my brother back to me, well, so be it.

Aurangzeb did say something that very deeply disturbed me. He said, "Sister, you know our grandfather Jahangir was as emperor called World Seizer, and when I am emperor I think I shall take the name of World Grasper. Is that not a fine name?" I was so shocked I could not answer. Aurangzeb will not be emperor. He is not the oldest. There are two sons ahead of him. How can he assume that he shall be emperor? My very silence must have revealed my thoughts. "You think I shall not be emperor?" he asked, raising his eyebrow. A peevish look hardened his face into that of the man.

"My dear brother, it is not in the order of things. Dara is older and then Shuja."

He cut me off, however, before I could finish my sentence. "But you shall support me, shall you not, sister?" There was a fire in his eyes and his face was bright with a terrifying illumination.

I honestly was not sure if what he said was a question or a threat. All I could wonder was if this indeed was the reason he had let me draw so close these last few days. Was he trying to buy my loyalty? "Brother," I replied, "I shall support our father and whomever our dear Aba feels should be emperor." "Our dear Aba." He practically spat the word out and turned his back, burying his head in the silk bolster.

November 25, 1628

I feel as if I am caught between two brothers. One with no heart learns the Koran by heart. The other with a heart, too large I do believe, learns the ancient Hindu text because he believes all men to be his brothers, whether Muslim or Hindu or Christian. One is supposed to be emperor and the other I believe would kill to be emperor.

So what am I to do with these two brothers? One thing is for certain: I must not tell Dara that Aurangzeb thinks he shall be emperor! This would cause an epic war within our own family. Besides, what can a princess, even a Princess of Princesses, do? We have no power. And yet it comes to me that there is one woman who has deadly power and that is Nur Mahal. Yes, it all makes sense now. Why would Aurangzeb meet with Nur Mahal, the woman who held him hostage and humiliated him when he was such a young child? Why? Because he is now firmly within her power. She did not need the Koh-i-Nor diamond to cast her spell. She merely promised him an empire. She promised him she would do anything to make him emperor.

I must see Panipat right away.

Later

Thank goodness. Panipat has done something about this situation. He will not tell me because he does not want to endanger me in any way. It is my belief that he has alerted my father, and that spies have been set upon Aurangzeb and Nur Mahal and perhaps even Samina and Raushanara. I shall rest better now.

November 26, 1628

Aurangzeb refuses to see me. This gives Raushanara great delight. He does grow better every day, however.

November 27, 1628

My peculiar dilemma — the brother dilemma — continues to plague me. I think I shall visit Indira's chambers. She is very wise and I must share this with someone. It is out of the question that I breathe a word of this to Ami.

Later

I have visited Indira and it was indeed a most astonishing, really surprising visit. I had requested to see her privately. We often go there to hear her stories of the Hindu epics and to learn a bit of Sanskrit. She received me quite formally. She seemed to know that I had something of great import to discuss. I love Indira's apartments, for she keeps several small shrines in little altars that are always adorned with flowers.

I began to tell of my dilemma and Indira listened most carefully. Indira wears a large ruby toe ring and when she began twisting it I knew she was really concentrating, for this is what she does when she thinks hard. Finally, she said to me, "Begum Sahib, much of what you say is not news to me. One only has to observe these two boys to note their differences, and especially with Aurangzeb. It is clear that this boy will do anything to become emperor." She paused, giving her toe ring a twist. "What disturbs me, Begum Sahib, is this notion of yours that we women of the harem have no power. Have you learned nothing in your almost fifteen years of life? Yes, it is true that we must keep purdah and sit veiled and screened to the rest of the world. But have we not become the keenest observers, the best listeners? And do you not think your father listens to us? Why, right now as we speak, your mother is in the Diwan-i-Khas, albeit behind a screen, but right next to the emperor as the petitioners come, the widows, the orphans, the scholars, or nobles. She listens to their pleas. And later the emperor will discuss them with her. And do you not notice that every time the emperor has a meeting with the gentlemen from the East India Company or if they are invited to sit at his table, he always asks me to be present behind the jalis? He knows that my father had many dealings with the factors, the commerce men of the East India Company, and was very clever. So he often asks me about his business dealings with the company."

So Indira said that we do have power and that it is the best kind — it is hidden. Then I heard the call for afternoon prayer, but she made me promise before I left that I shall accompany her tomorrow to the durbar when my father meets with representatives of the East India Company. She told me that I must sit right by her, for she will have the seat with the best view through the screen of the gentlemen and the meetings.

November 28, 1628

I am very tired this evening. I have followed Indira about all day long and tried to listen as she listens. It has been a lesson! When we went to the durbar I sat right next to her behind the screen, which gave me a perfect view of the gentlemen from the East India Company — and I could hear, too! My first thought was how pink all those Englishmen look. I had never seen their skin up close before. Some of them had orange spots and one had bright red hair. Redder than Queen Elizabeth's. I would hate to be such a color. I, of course, did not understand their speech because I do not speak English, but the translator had a very distinct and loud voice. Indira said my father always uses him when the company comes to visit. At first it seemed boring and nothing unusual. Then the gentlemen asked about "liberty of traffic and privileges" for what they described as the "benefits of both kingdoms." I saw Indira's face crease deeply into a frown, and she made a small tapping noise on the jalis with her long, painted fingernails. Immediately a servant of one of my father's councilors came over.

"Ask him, 'What benefits?'" she hissed through the screen. The servant went back to the secretary, who whispered to my father's most distinguished general, Khan Jahan Lodi. I saw the general smile broadly and nod toward the screen as if he could almost see Indira. He then went to my father. General Lodi is one of my father's most trusted advisers. I saw my father nod vigorously in agreement with the general and then look toward the jalis as if he, too, could see Indira. Then I saw Indira's sneer as the gentlemen's response was translated. Once more the servant came back, this time with General Lodi, and I heard Indira say, "Tell them we want the British ships to protect our pilgrim ships to Mecca."

<u>What a good idea,</u> I thought. Every year many noblemen of my father's court fulfill their Muslim duty by visiting Mecca, and every year it seems that Dutch ships attack them. It was in that moment that I began to understand the power of the harem. Here is Indira, not even a Muslim, caged in the lacy shadows of the pierced screens of purity, silent and unseen, and yet she was driving a bargain that could save lives, lives of the nobles of my father's court. And my Aba listened to her. He listened to my mother when the petitioners came. And perhaps he will one day listen to me.

I shall make a point this evening to discuss with Ami the decisions she helped Aba make for the petitioners.

December 5, 1628

There has been another addition to the company of the little wives — a Christian woman! Ami tells me that my great-grandfather Akbar also had a Christian wife from the country of Armenia. I am not sure where this one is from. But is it not wonderful that Aba tries so hard to follow in the footsteps of the glorious Akbar?

Needless to say Aurangzeb has been sulking.

December 6, 1628

The new wife's name is Alafara. She is very pretty and although dark in complexion has green eyes exactly the color of jade. And she knows chess! I want to learn how to play chess, and Ami says she will ask Alafara to teach me.

December 9, 1628

Samina is such an elephant nose! She pokes into everything. She sent a message through her eunuch Ali to Aba that Alafara was to teach me chess and she felt it was improper for a little wife to be in such contact with a Begum Sahib. Now poor Aba is caught. He feels that perhaps Samina is right (I don't see the sense of this at all) but that she was out of place in sending him the message and not first discussing it with Ami or at least Indira. It is very poor form for a number four wife to jump ahead and assert her opinion without first consulting a number one or number two wife.

December 10, 1628

The dispute is settled. I am to learn chess from Alafara in the presence of Ami and Satty. This apparently makes it an acceptable "lesson."

December 12, 1628

Chess is hard! I think that Alafara is very intelligent. It is as if she can keep all the positions where I could possibly move chessmen in her head all at once and anticipate whatever I do.

December 16, 1628

Alafara explained about the Christian god and his son Jesus, who died on the cross for all people's sins. "Even mine?" I blurted out. Everybody seemed to think this was very funny and laughed. I hate it when people laugh like that at me. Was it such a stupid question? I mean, I am a Muslim — should Jesus die for me? Then Ami sensed my embarrassment and said, "Janni, dear, I do not believe you have any sins." Well, this surprised me, too. How would she know? And am I so simple that I can have no sin or appear to have no sins? She does not know, I warrant, my bad thoughts about Aurangzeb. I must conclude that if people believe I have no sins I must be a very uninteresting person.

December 17, 1628

I am bored. It is probably because I am uninteresting. But I started thinking yesterday after our discussion of sin. If I have no sins, I began to think, it is probably because I have not had the opportunity to commit one. I cannot marry, therefore I cannot be unfaithful to a husband. I cannot rule, therefore I could not be a bad empress like Nur Mahal even if I wanted to. But then my thinking begins to whirl around in circles: does one have to be sinful to be interesting? Yet another dilemma in my life.

December 18, 1628

I am still bored. The days grow short in this winter season but the nights seem long, as we no longer can have our meals in the garden. And I prefer music outdoors and can listen forever. Both Indira and Ami urge me to attend the durbars and the private audiences of the emperor but I often doze off. Aba is planning a new city in Delhi. It is rumored that it will be the new capital. I hear him talking to the royal architects about where to put a great mosque, and he dreams of a great tree-shaded avenue and a fort and another royal mosque that he wants to be made of white marble. He is already calling it the Pearl Mosque. I would love to plan a great city, to decide where the mosques go and where the gates of the city should be and to dream of fountains and avenues and plazas. Yes, Aba says there shall be a plaza that he shall call the Moonlight Plaza. Oh, to be an emperor and never bored!

I look at the small miniature portrait of Queen

Elizabeth that I wear around my neck and study her very white, narrow face with her nearly pink hair fuzzing about it. I do not know if she ever built a city, but she fought wars. She defeated what was thought to be the greatest navy in the entire world, the Spanish Armada. Satty told me all about it. She made laws. And she never was married and I bet she was <u>never</u> bored.

December 19, 1628

I have a solution to my dilemma — not the sin part, the boring part. I am going to ask Aba for my birthday if we might hold a Flirting Bazaar like the one where he met Ami. There has not been one in several years, apparently, because last year we were all in the Deccan where Aba was fighting the rebellious Rajputs, and for several years before then my grandfather Jahangir was too sick and Nur Mahal had reduced the festivities of the court.

December 20, 1628

There is to be a Flirting Bazaar! I am so excited. Aba thought it was a wonderful idea.

Later

Aurangzeb is furious. He thinks a Flirting Bazaar is an offense to women. Hah! Even Raushanara is excited. She came to me and very sweetly asked what goods we should trade in. She wants to do fine embroideries and brocades. But I said, "Nonsense — if you want to meet young gentlemen we should have a turban booth. Panipat knows all the latest turban styles and he will help us gather them." She agreed! Her eyes shone and she said, "Janni, how clever you are!"

Another thought: wouldn't it be funny if out of this entire Flirting Bazaar all I get is my sister back?

December 21, 1628

Aurangzeb went to Aba and tried to talk him out of the Flirting Bazaar. But Aba was so clever. He said to Aurangzeb, "Let us find a special celebration that you would enjoy." So it has been decided that just after the Flirting Bazaar we shall travel to Fatehpur Sikri to honor the Muslim Saint Salim Chisti, to whom that mosque is dedicated. He is quite happy, and then Ami had the wonderful idea of allowing Aurangzeb to participate in the planning of the Pearl Mosque in the new city of Delhi. This indeed was a stroke of genius. I cannot believe how smart my Ami is. Oh, if I could be as smart and as beautiful and as kind as Ami!

Ami says she will let Raushanara and I do all the planning for our booth at the Flirting Bazaar. Indira is getting a bit elephant nosy about the whole thing, offering a few too many suggestions, but Ami always says, "Indira, let them do it themselves."

I think Ami understands not just girls but me in a way no other human being on Earth ever could. I do not know what I would do without Ami. I know it would be wonderful if Ami had another baby, but quite honestly, part of me always dreads finding out she is expecting. She has had six children but has lost seven before childbirth. She always seems to regain her strength. But what if the next time she does not? What if something should happen to her?

December 22, 1628

Only twelve more days until the Flirting Bazaar. Only nine until my birthday. But I'm much more excited about the bazaar.

December 23, 1628

Something terrible has happened. Panipat lies near death. He has been poisoned. I know who did this. I am sure. If Panipat dies I shall kill Nur Mahal.

December 24, 1628

I pray to Allah but Panipat grows weaker and weaker. I know this sounds silly to say but if Allah would permit Panipat to live I would give up the Flirting Bazaar and never think twice of it again. I would.

December 25, 1628

Dare I hope? Panipat has taken a turn for the better.

December 29, 1628

It is a miracle. Panipat lives! And I shall keep my promise. I care for no bazaars.

Later

I was so excited about Panipat but then in the middle of the night it came to me: If Panipat has survived this attack, surely Nur Mahal will plan another. I could not sleep. I have done something I have never in my life done. I sent Jumpha to tell the guards of my father's bedchamber that I must see him right away. Aba came running to me with Ami. They thought I was sick. I told them that I could not come this close again to losing Panipat. I told them of my fears of Nur Mahal, and then Ami and Aba exchanged long looks. Finally Aba spoke, "My dear child, Nur Mahal has been placed under palace arrest. Do not fear."

I said, "Aba can't you simply send her away?"

And he said, "Never. She must be watched constantly." I felt that something was left unsaid. And I think what was left unsaid was, "And so, too, must Aurangzeb be watched constantly." But of course it must be very hard for a father to say this about his own child, especially to another one of his children.

December 30, 1628

It is so odd how one's view of things changes after having gone through a terrible time like Panipat's nearly dying. I truly do not care about the Flirting Bazaar. It is not just that I made a promise to Allah never to think about it again. I simply do not care. But everyone else does! Even Panipat. We are to come to his chambers, where a turban maker shall bring his wares and display them. Panipat can advise from his bed, as he is still too weak to be up for long.

January 2, 1629

Today is my birthday. I am fifteen. I have grown much taller. Ami measured me. I would like to know how tall Queen Elizabeth was when she was fifteen. This woman of late has begun to haunt my thoughts. I want to know more about her. She had a sister who was very troublesome, very religious, and who was queen before Elizabeth. I guess Elizabeth was not so religious. This angered the sister. She even had Elizabeth imprisoned. But she survived. I think about how I have this strangely religious brother. Does it not seem strange that God should come between brothers and sisters? Would my brother ever imprison me? What a terrible thought.

Aba gave me a diamond ankle bracelet and a new elephant! This elephant is an immense female. But it is remarkable how gracefully and smoothly she moves. I have watched her walk from the courtyard and I have ridden on her now in my howdah. Never have I experienced such a movement. Her steps are liquid and it is as if I am in a boat gliding on a calm lake. I am thinking of calling her Natya, which is the Sanskrit word for dance. I shall ride her in the celebration in Fatehpur Sikri for the Muslim saint later this month. And I am instructing my mahout that whenever we go out she must be garlanded in jasmine just like the Bharata Natayam dancers. I think I shall order various of the mudra hand gestures to be painted on her trunk.

Later

I took Murad, because he so loves the elephants, along with me today while Panipat relayed my instructions to the mahouts for the dressing of Natya. She is going to look simply splendid. Aba has presented her with an apron of solid gold studded with rubies to wear on her immense forehead. As I write, several servant girls are weaving nearly a thousand jasmine blossoms to swag over her sides and loop up onto my howdah. Her flanks will be painted with the mudra hand gestures along with other decorative designs, and I have ordered tinkly silver bells just like the ones the dancers wear to fringe my howdah.

January 3, 1629

Raushanara and I went to Panipat's chambers today to view the turbans for our booth. Indira came as well. She was full of suggestions. Ami has promised to stay out of sight of our booth. I am not sure if the same can be said for Indira!

January 5, 1629

It was all over so fast! I cannot believe how quickly it went. But Aba promises us another one next year. I shall start counting the days tomorrow, I know. The bazaar was everything I ever hoped for, but you know, I am still not sure exactly what flirting is. I almost got a sense one time. It was when a gentleman from the East India Company came over. But wait, I am rushing too fast through my story. I want to savor every minute of the bazaar from the very first when we came into the great hall when it was still empty of most people and we began to set up our booths.

Oh it was so much fun. We were just like shop girls. Panipat had found small wooden stands to set our turbans on for display and Ami had brought some fine brocade for us to drape on the tables. Indira had brought us a lovely little jeweled casket to use to keep the rupees in that we collected from our sales. With the help of the artists from the painting studios we had signs advertising our goods. Then, of course, Indira had to poke her nose in and tell us how to keep our prices up. "When they offer you a lower price you must cast your eyes down and say, 'Oh, sir, that is an insult.' Remember girls, you must use the word 'insult' a lot. That will shame them into offering more. And when they say, 'What is the best you can do?' you never, never give them an answer. You say, 'What is the best you can do?' And then they name a price and you double it."

But I am not sure about the casting-the-eyes-down part. How would a gentleman ever see our eyes? Even though on this special occasion we were permitted to come out from behind the screens, we wore our heaviest veils.

Still it was much fun. We had been working at least an

hour and I had already sold many fine turbans when a gentleman from the East India Company came by. I was not really sure he was English, for he spoke excellent Persian and he was not that funny pink color that all English people seem to be. He was dark of skin but had yellow hair and bright blue eyes. It was most curious. He did not look as if he was from our world, but he spoke without a trace of an accent. We had a pale blue-and-silver turban with a peacock feather that I thought would look quite handsome on him. So I presented it. He began to speak and to try it on. I told him that although he might speak flawless Persian he knew nothing about wearing a turban, for he had it perched at a silly angle. I could not believe I said that! My own words shocked me. I had spoken so boldly. I felt my skin flush under the veil, and I was almost about to apologize. But then I caught a twinkling in his eyes and I forgot all about apologizing. I wanted to say something else to make those blue eyes dance. I had never seen such blue eyes, the sharpest blue, like the licks of blue flame in a sapphire. And I felt some tiny flame flicker in me. Deep inside me there was a quivering. He dipped his head and asked me to adjust the turban.

Raushanara giggled and I heard a raucous laugh from Indira — who was not supposed to be there. I knew, of course, that I could not touch him. So I took a step back and whispered, "No my lord." But I brushed aside my veil slightly by moving my shoulder. And I think, no, I know that he saw the curve of my cheek and a bit of my eye, which I daresay sparkled as fiercely as his my dark amber eye, his fierce blue gemstone eye.

I think this is flirting. I think this quivering I felt and still feel whenever I think of him is part of the flirting.

January 6, 1629

I think of nothing but the yellow-haired Englishman with the sapphire eyes. I am determined to attend every durbar and audience in which the gentlemen of the East India Company are in attendance. Perhaps I shall see him again. I do not even know his name!

January 8, 1629

I have a terrible feeling someone has been reading the pages of this diary. The thought first came to me several days before the Flirting Bazaar. I have become increasingly suspicious. I notice small things that are out of the usual order in my apartments. I keep the diary in a lacquered box. It has a lock, but it is a simple one. And now I realize that there are probably scores of such boxes in the palace and that it would be easy to obtain a key that might fit any one of them. And I think that is just what has happened. I think someone has found a key that works — but not so perfectly. Yes, the key opens the box but the lock plate is now askew as if the person had to jiggle the key hard. It was never that way before.

I cannot describe the awful feeling with which this has left me. Someone has intruded into my most private thoughts. I feel violated in the most profound way. I have no desire to even write in this diary anymore, even though Panipat says he can obtain for me an absolutely secure box with an unbreakable lock. For now I do not think I can write. I feel so exposed. I hate that someone has read about the quivering I felt for the blue-eyed Englishman. I hate that in this diary I have betrayed petty thoughts about Indira that others might have read. I hate that I cannot entertain quietly and alone my fears concerning Aurangzeb, and my doubts about his passion for Allah. I hate that someone else knows of the tenderness and love that I feel for Ami. These are my thoughts, and although some of them might not be good thoughts, they are nonetheless MINE. MINE! MINE! MINE! Is it not bad enough that I must live in the world of purdah behind screens of purity, forever veiled, locked in a cage of lace shadows that despite their prettiness might as well be iron bars? Must I now lock away my very thoughts, the life's breath of my brain, my very soul in a zenana of the mind? This is the last I shall write for a long, long time.

December 5, 1629
Agra

After all these months of peace when we had finally begun to accustom ourselves to the pleasant rhythms of court life — summer and autumn in Srinagar, winter and spring in the Agra palace — these agreeable cadences of life have been interrupted. Aba has just been informed that General Khan Jahan Lodi has defected to the south with seven thousand horses and men in addition to fifty elephants. It is feared that he will join forces with the ruler of Bijapur, the very ruler who kept us imprisoned in the Deccan two years ago. Together they would make a powerful rebel coalition. This seems unbelievable to me. General Lodi was my father's most trusted general. They had been friends since childhood. He is related to Tali, my father's first wife. This could make things very bad for Tali. But for now it is bad for all of us, for we must once more set out for the Deccan. Aba feels that he must present himself to the people of this territory.

There is a quietness in the entire palace tonight. I play a game of chess with Alafara and no one even seems to notice that neither Satty nor Ami is present. Such concerns of a Begum Sahib playing a game with a little wife seem trivial now. Aurangzeb has gone to the mosque to pray and I suppose I should rejoice in the fact that Dara has been invited to attend a council in the Ghusl Khana. This is surely a sign that Aba intends for Dara to succeed him as emperor. Dara has grown so tall and handsome in this past year. Ami has even thought of a brilliant match for him. Her notion of the perfect bride is Nadira Begum, the daughter of Aba's late half brother Prince Parwiz. Aba was so happy that he had already sent out the first batch of orders to begin preparations for an imperial wedding two years from now when Dara is sixteen. Nadira was supposed to come and live with us in the harem. But now, because we must set off once more on a campaign, she will not. This is all terribly disappointing and most of all to Dara, for he has met Nadira on many occasions and is very taken with her.

We leave for the Deccan in less than a week.

December 23, 1629
Deccan territory

We entered the Deccan territory last night. It is just as I remembered it. Stark slabs of dark lava jagged at the edges give it a forbidding appearance. Old riverbeds and stream channels are dry and dusty, their usual state except for a few days of the year when they might flow with thick, black-looking water. Rocky humps and lava formations boil up from the ground to occasionally interrupt the flatness. We must keep watch now for the Maratha bands. Aba calls the Marathas the devil's spawn, for these fierce tribes live in the isolated valleys and mountains surrounding the Deccan and are capable of sweeping down onto the Deccan plateau in the blink of an eye and annihilating a unit of cavalry- or infantrymen. Aba says one must never underestimate a Maratha. They appear crude but they are clever. They look small but are wiry and have enormous strength. They are Hindus and claim to be *Kshatriyas* — the warrior breed of Hindus — and indeed they live for war. They are brutal, and unlike the Rajput princes, whom Aba must sometimes fight, they have no codes of honor and cherish no notions of nobility.

Indira says they are not Kshatriyas at all, but "mere thugs."

We have been en route for almost ten days now. I was pleased today because for the first time Dara came and shared my howdah atop Natya. I think he shall come back more often now that he knows of Natya's almost magical gait. He rides with a unit of cavalry. There are more than five hundred horsemen in just this one unit. Every few days Aba has him change divisions. On some days he is required to walk with the infantry. I would not have thought Dara would like this at all, but he is quite fond of the commander of this unit, Wazir Beg, who, it turns out, is a Sufi Muslim, like my brother. I began to giggle, for I imagine my poetic, philosophical brother wandering about, exchanging mystical thoughts with Commander Beg as they lead their troops perhaps in circles. Dara thought this was terribly funny, too. We shared a good laugh over this. And this has led me in turn to a sudden revelation. I think the reason Dara and I are so close is not because we share deep philosophical thoughts, although I am as intrigued as he is by the notions of the Sufis, but because we think the same things are funny. Yes, I suppose that seems ridiculous. But it is really our beliefs in what is funny and not our beliefs in Allah that draw us together. It is indeed the comic rather than the cosmic. One of my very first memories — I could not have been more than four and Dara three — was when we got into Indira's *bindi* box and pasted bindi spots all over our faces. We both thought this was so funny we did not even cry when we were punished. We just laughed the entire time Satty made us "go to the Deccan" — yes, that is what they called the punishment when we were removed from the common chambers of the zenana and sent to a special little silk tent near the eunuch quarters. We had to sit there until we had sufficiently thought about our transgressions and were called back. We were not called back for hours because we were laughing the entire time and hardly displaying signs of being contrite.

And now we really do go to the Deccan. It is so nice that we can still laugh.

December 24, 1629
Deccan territory

Dara came again today to my howdah. He said Natya is becoming irresistible. I said, "What about me?" Again we laughed. Dara brought with him diagrams he has copied that show the organization of the army. I think this is what distracts him from thoughts of Nadira. In any case he showed me the diagrams. There are ten thousand cavalrymen and three thousand infantrymen. Then there are thousands of matchlockmen with their rifles and archers, and spearmen as well. We collect them as we pass through the territories of various Hindu princes and Rajputs. Dara is trying to memorize the commanders of each division and wanted me to quiz him on them. I found this very boring after a few minutes and changed the topic of discussion to his wedding. He said it is so far off he cannot imagine it. But I said I can, because Ami told me all about her wedding to Aba.

January 2, 1630
Deccan territory

I turned sixteen today. I thought it would be very dismal having my birthday as we travel south. But Ami made a special event of it. I do not know how she ever did this but somehow in this forsaken land she managed to provide julabmost. It was a complete surprise to me. We had been under way since dawn, and just after noon when we had stopped for prayers, Ami's servant announced that the empress wished to visit. So the silver ladder was brought and first came the servant with the gold dome platter, then another with another platter, and then Ami followed by Satty and Dara and Aba — Aba with the dust of the road still on his face, for he had been riding at the head of the cavalry. But they had brought a birthday feast right into my howdah. When they uncovered the first dish I saw at least eight or nine bowls of my favorite flavors of Julab-most — apricot, pomegranate, rosewater, orange. And then there were tiny sweet cakes and when I bit into one Ami said, "Be careful." My teeth struck something hard and out popped a huge star sapphire! It is Ami's star sapphire, the one she was given on her sixteenth birthday, and she wants me to have it. I protested. I cannot help but think of the gentleman from the East India Company with the sapphire eyes.

"You are my precious jewel, daughter," Ami replied, but in her eyes I saw something sad. I wonder if she is thinking that because I am a Begum Sahib I shall never be able to know the kind of love she has found and shared with my father. My mother is too smart to think that a mere jewel can replace or compensate for that kind of love, but I think she wants me to know that she recognizes this fate of mine. For that reason alone this star sapphire will become my most precious possession, I do believe. And this birthday, that I thought would be so dismal, I think is my happiest. My Ami has brought me julabmost and precious jewels. I must not ask for more.

January 10, 1630

The Marathas are not the only thing we have to fear. As we pass farther into the Deccan we see signs of the great famine that has plagued the countryside. The scenes from my howdah are unbearable to watch. We see desolate villages that appear scorched from a drought that has finished all their crops. They appear at first like ghost towns, but then we encounter along the highways the inhabitants, skeletal, their eyes fixed and staring as if they are already dead. Indeed they seem like the walking dead. However, they might suddenly come to life if they spot a dung heap. They scramble to the excrement left by oxen or their sacred cows and pick through it for undigested seeds and grain. Today I saw one man take out a knife and slash the throat of another as they argued over the contents of a dunghill. A few minutes later I saw a mother offering her child for sale for a few rupees, and then I saw another giving her child away to anyone who would take him. The baby's stomach was as swollen as I have ever seen before. I do not understand why, when a child is starving, its belly swells. But its limbs were like little twigs.

January 11, 1630

I cannot get the images of these starving babies out of my mind. Every day the road becomes thicker with people begging for food. Aba has sent special fast-riding couriers ahead to Burhanpur and ordered ox carts laden with grain to be sent to this region.

January 15, 1630

I do not believe what I have just done. But in my lap I hold a baby girl. Her eyes are gummy. Her stomach is swollen. Jumpha goes in search of Mirza. Mirza is a wet nurse of the harem. There are always at least three wet nurses in case my mother should give birth. Mirza is the best. Am I a fool to have done this? No one knows of it except Jumpha and me. I looked down from my howdah and saw this woman with stick arms holding up a baby. I don't know why but I just couldn't stand it. The little baby looked up at me and despite her gummy eyes I thought I saw them focus. They did not have the death light of so many of the babies I have seen. I thought perhaps there might be a chance to save at least this little one. I did not know if it was a girl or a boy. Now I know. It is a girl. But she looks more like a little old woman. There is something almost birdlike about her. I wipe her eyes with a soft cloth dipped in rosewater. She opens them wider and looks at me. She looks too wise for her age. What is that age? Maybe six months, maybe less. I poke the tip of my finger into her mouth. Her suck is weak. Oh, live, little bird! Live!

Later

Allah be praised! Jumpha found Mirza. Mirza says she must teach the baby to suck properly, for it is so long since she has nursed. First she squirted breast milk onto her finger and wiped it gently inside the baby's mouth. I saw the baby's little tongue poke out a bit. Mirza said that is a good sign.

Still later

The baby has begun to suck just a little bit! We also dip clean cloths into water and squeeze them into the baby's mouth, for Mirza says the baby is too dry. She can tell this from looking at the baby's urine. She did not even wear a diaper when she came. I hold the baby and do this. I like having something helpful to do. The baby looks up at me with those large, almost knowing dark eyes. "Little baby," I whisper, "who are you?" And suddenly a name for this baby comes to me. Jaytayu, the wise and wonderful bird from the epic story of the Ramayana.

Her wise little eyes peer out at me, her brow crinkles. She has seen so much, too much within this one life she has led. It is a most terrible thing to lose one's mother but if a promise of new life can be made . . . Oh, suck, little baby, grow strong, and I shall try to protect you forever.

January 17, 1630

I knew we could not keep Jaytayu a secret. But thankfully all have fallen in love with her. She sucks well now and Ami is most enchanted with her. Her little hollow cheeks have filled out a bit, I believe, and her eyes sparkle each time she is put to the breast. I love her dearly. I wrap her in gold-embroidered coverlets. Ami thinks she is about six months old. Aba, too, is quite taken with her. He calls her Jay Jay for short.

January 18, 1630

Troublesome news has arrived here. It is reported that Khan Jahan Lodi has been joined by the notorious Deccan rebel Raja Jujhar Singh Bundela.

Later

Worse news: it is rumored that the Maratha warriors have joined these rebels. An imperial detachment of twenty thousand cavalrymen and forty thousand infantrymen, and many units of matchlock soldiers as well, leave tonight. They are under the command of three of Aba's most skillful and loyal generals: Khan Dawran, Abdullah Khan, and Sayidd Jahan Barha.

But what if these generals suddenly defect? I am frightened and I can tell from Ami's grave face that she is as well. For years my dear mother has followed my father on campaigns. I do not think one ever becomes accustomed to war. Ami has been pregnant thirteen times in all, and mostly it has been on the campaign trail that she has given birth or miscarried.

January 21, 1630

I am so scared. The enemy is much closer than anyone thought. They are perhaps as near as three *kos*. From our encampment we can hear the shudders of the earth under the feet of thousands of elephants.

There is a sound that I have never forgotten, or will ever forget. It is the sound of the Elephant Walk — the sound of skulls being crushed by the feet of elephants, of a face caving in as the elephant plants its immense foot squarely on the head of a wounded person. And for the elephant it is no different than setting its foot on a coconut. Once before when I was a very little girl, the enemy's troops came close, and I can remember the sound of our cavalrymen's heads turned to a bloody mash in the dirt. I cup my hand around Jay Jay's little skull with its fine, downy black hair. What crevice could we hide in? Where might we go? I shall dream of elephants' feet, I know.

Later

In the middle of the night I am awakened by an acrid smell. When I peek out of the tent I see that the black of the night has become smudged. Clouds of smoke roll up on the horizon. Ami comes to my chamber. Her face is no longer grave but quick and intense with an almost joyous anticipation.

"It is an old trick, Janni, and this is why it pays to study the diaries of the past emperors."

"Akbar?" I ask. She shakes her head, no. Next I ask if it was my great-great-great-grandfather Babur. Once again she shakes her head. I am confounded. "Timur," Ami replied. Timur! The first of the Moghul invaders.

Ami explained to me that Aba commanded his generals to use an old technique that Timur had practiced to cause panic among the enemy. The ground was planted with stakes with upward spikes and the cavalry was fitted with *caltrops,* a similar instrument. A horseman could entice an elephant to follow him and then scatter these deadly barbs. But another device was even more effective and it was used as well. Carts with bundles of burning grasses are rolled toward the elephants and the elephants flee in panic. It was the burning grasses and carts I was smelling.

Soon enough we were hearing enormous thuds as elephants crashed into one another or collapsed in piles onto the earth. The embroidered flaps of my tent quivered with the tremors of falling elephants.

January 22, 1630

It is victory. Aba greeted the triumphant generals this morning. The generals presented the heads of the traitors to my father in a ceremony. But the worst of the traitors, Khan Jahan Lodi, has escaped, so it is felt that it is not yet safe to leave the Deccan.

Oh, I am weary of this campaign. I long for our quiet life. How I would love to return to Kashmir and our garden palace there. How I would love to show my little Jay Jay Silver Island of Lake Dal and lead her to the shrine of Krishna.

May 15, 1631
Deccan, capital city of Burhanpur

I have dared not write for all this time for fear that writing would somehow bring bad luck to Ami. You see, she desperately wanted to have another baby and for months did not conceive. Then when she finally did it was as if no one dared speak of it because we were all fearful she might miscarry. But now it is such a joy to see Ami. She swells bigger with each day. Doctor Wazir thinks the baby should come within three weeks. We are all so excited. I tease little Jay Jay that she will no longer be the baby. She must share her toys. She has a special doll she calls Big Baby. So I tell her another Big Baby is coming. She speaks many words now. "Big Baby" are two. And she calls me Mi Mi. I think it is supposed to be Ami. She walks now although I do not know how she learned, since we have been on the campaign most of the past year. But we have at last settled in Burhanpur, the seat of Aba's government for the Deccan. The palace here is not nearly so nice as the one in Agra, but Aba is busy making improvements already and talking with his architect. Although most of them are still busy with the design of the new capital in Delhi, Aba hopes construction shall start soon. There is a large East India Company warehouse here as Burhanpur is on the trading route. I have seen through the jalis screens much of the blue-eyed Englishman that I "flirted" with at the bazaar, which now seems so long ago. I have now found out that his name is Peter Mundy. Many people call him Honest Peter Mundy because he is considered a man of great fairness and integrity. He is a special favorite of Aba's, and Aba often invites him to ceremonies and entertainments. I can often see him at these occasions from my position behind the screens, and sometimes I feel as if he knows precisely where I am sitting and that he can sense my watching him. He often writes in a book. Perhaps he is keeping a record just as Abdul-Hamid Lahawri keeps a diary of my father's reign. I wonder if I am mentioned in Honest Peter Mundy's diary.

May 26, 1631

It is indeed Peter Mundy who brings us news from the front now, just as he did last February when at last Khan Jahan Lodi was captured and killed. Now there is more good news. The siege of the fort of Qandahar was a success. Nasri Khan led the imperial forces and the fort was successfully blown up. I think Aba bought the gunpowder from the East India Company. Even after it was blown up our foot soldiers had to lay siege and there was much valiant fighting, according to Peter Mundy. Today at the durbar I saw Mr. Mundy sitting with the court painter Payag, describing the siege to him so he might paint the depiction for my father's diary.

June 1, 1631

Ami looks quite tired today. Jay Jay was a bit too much for her, too rambunctious. So Jumpha took her away. Aurangzeb is preparing for Ramadan. He begins his preparations by eating less each day. I would not have the discipline, and although he encourages Raushanara, she certainly does not have the discipline. She has become quite plump and, I might add, even more sullen than usual. This will be the first Ramadan where Murad will have to fast. He is old enough now to do a half day. That is how Ami starts the children on their fasting. I just wish that the baby would come before Ramadan. I hate to think of Ami having to fast. Thank goodness two of the wet nurses are Hindu and will not have to fast. Milk produced by fasting women is not thought to be as rich.

June 5, 1631

I spend much time in Ami's apartments. She talks a lot about Dara's wedding. A specific date, of course, has not been set because the astrologers are still consulting. It most likely shall be sometime in January or February, depending on the transit of the stars.

June 10, 1631

The days are unbearably hot and Ramadan begins tomorrow and still my mother waits for this child. Doctor Wazir thinks it should have arrived by now.

I play with Jay Jay in the pools all morning. She loves to stand under the fountains. I think Jay Jay loves julab-most as much as I do. Indira is teaching her a Hindu song with hand movements. Of course, she is too young to really learn it, but she keeps saying, whenever Indira stops, "More, more." Indira has great patience. It is too bad she has never had a child of her own. Right now I almost wish she were having this one for Ami. Ami looks so pale.

June 15, 1631

My mother has been taken into the birthing apartments. My father sits with her constantly. He receives no dignitaries. All audiences are canceled. Everyone wants this child to come so much.

Later

I see Doctor Wazir and his assistants and women of the harem knowledgeable in the matters of birth coming and going. They all have very worried expressions. I am not allowed in.

June 16, 1631

Things do not go well with Ami. I must be allowed in to see my mother.

I see in the courtyard astrologers hovering over their astrolabes and charts. They are trying to figure which stars will influence what all hope is a princely birth. I just hope myself for a birth. I care not whether the babe is a girl or boy. I should not write this but I really do not care if the babe dies. I only want my mother to live. I can hear her cries from here. They must let me in.

Later

Blessed Indira. She went to my father and asked that I be allowed into the birthing apartment. I go now.

Still later

It was a shock to see my mother's face. It did not seem like her at all. Her eyes were unfocused. I do not think she recognized me, though I held her hand and whispered, "Ami, Ami, it is me, your Janni."

She cannot die. I thought once that my father had died and still he lived. I thought my dear Panipat would die and promised Allah never to think of the Flirting Bazaar if he would live. Allah, what might I promise you now? I would promise you anything for my mother's life.

June 17, 1631

It is four hours before dawn. My mother fades.

An hour later

My mother suddenly became alert. Her eyes focused. It was so strange. "Janni, call your father," my mother shrieked.

And then with a torrent of blood my sister was born. Aba arrived just in time. Ami opened her eyes and spoke directly to my father. The words made no sense to me. "Take care, dear one, of our children and this little one . . . good-bye."

Ami has died. It has been three hours since she passed over. I cannot believe that I and my Ami no longer are both on this same planet called Earth. The world feels empty to me. The zenana quivers with the lamentations and the high drone of keening. Bursting through this wall of tears are my father's ferocious sobs. Many sit and recite the Koran, the bleak verses on the promised afterlife, of a garden even more beautiful than the ones my father and grandfather created on Earth.

The washers now go to my mother's apartment. These are women who know the art of preparing a body for eternity. They shall wash Ami in cold camphor water. They will wrap her in five pieces of white cotton. They will carry her away, since ghosts are much dreaded, and when they do, they shall carry her headfirst. They will carry her this way because they believe the spirit will not find its way back. But I would welcome my mother's ghost. I would run to greet and hug her.

June 24, 1631

It has been a week since Ami died and this morning I woke suddenly hours before dawn, indeed the same hour as when my mother died. It was not a dream that woke me, but a thought. And with that thought I could swear I heard Ami's voice.

But I am not frightened. I am joyous. Joyous with realization. For I cannot help but think what a lucky person I am. Imagine that in all the eons of time, in all the possible universes of which Dara speaks, of all the stars in the heavens, Ami and I came together for one brief and shining sliver of time. I stop. I think. Supposing in the grand infinity of this universe two particles of life, Ami and me, swirl endlessly like grains of sand in the oceans of the world — how much of a chance is there for these two particles, these two grains of sand, to collide, to rest briefly together on the same beach, at the same moment in time?

That is what happened with Ami and me. I praise Allah for this miracle of chance. It was a divine gamble that made me my mother's daughter. And if, as the Hindus believe, we are reincarnated, I do not care if I am a princess or my mother is an empress. I would be a ragged, half-naked babe if only my Ami would once again be my mother. That is all the richness I shall ever need. Indeed there would be a splendor to my life no gold could ever match.

Epilogue

After her mother's death, Jahanara served as the un-crowned empress of the Moghul empire. In 1644, however, Jahanara came very close to dying in a terrible fire when her perfumed robes caught the flame of a candle. Shah Jahan himself nursed her night and day until she recovered, which was some months later.

Shah Jahan did not die until 1666. His last years were profoundly sad ones. Aurangzeb indeed was determined to be emperor, and in pursuit of this destiny he rose up against his brothers, killing the Crown Prince Dara. He declared himself emperor. As part of his strategy, he imprisoned his own father in the palace at Agra, confining him to apartments in the white marble buildings that Shah Jahan had designed for his harem. From the windows of his quarters, the deposed emperor could view the tomb of his beloved wife.

Eight years after the death of the empress, an immense

pearl floated up into an azure sky. It was the dome of the Taj Mahal, Shah Jahan's magnificent memorial to the love of his life, his wife Mumtaz Mahal. It has been called the most beautiful and the most mysteriously romantic building in the world. Begun within months of her death, it was not completely finished until 1648, almost twenty years later. Its original name was Rauza-i-Munavvara, which meant Tomb of Light, but it became better known as the Taj Mahal, a name derived from the empress's own name. It has been called a dream of white marble. The perfection of the building is unmatched in its design and use of materials. It is truly a work of love, and as a Bengali poet wrote, *"Only let this one teardrop, the Taj Mahal, glisten on the cheek of time for ever and ever."*

Shah Jahan's Peacock Throne was another example of his lavish taste. Completed in 1635, the throne was made entirely of gold and encrusted with jewels. It was the most magnificent throne ever created for a ruler. In 1739, the emperor of Persia stole the throne from India and took it back to Persia where it served as the throne until the fall of the Persian monarchy in 1979. The last emperor to sit on the Peacock Throne was the Shah Mohammed Reza Pahlavi of Iran.

During Shah Jahan's last years he was cared for by his favorite daughter, Jahanara. He and his son never reconciled. When Shah Jahan died he was buried next to his wife in the Taj Mahal.

Jahanara never married. She devoted her life largely to writing and painting and composing poetry. She became more deeply interested in the study of the mystical Sufi saints of Islam. For some years after Jahanara's father died, Raushanara — impetuous, sharp-tongued, and as hungry for power as her brother — superseded Jahanara in position and power in the court. At this point, it appears that Jahanara abandoned the Agra Palace and went to the new capital of Delhi that her father had built. There she enjoyed an extensive amount of freedom — perhaps even more freedom than her sister Raushanara.

Raushanara petitioned her brother to allow her to live outside the palace, as Jahanara now did. Aurangzeb, who had become even more puritanical and austere, was shocked by her request for freedom and is said to have replied that his love for her would not allow him to permit her to leave, for he needed her to train his own daughters in the proper conduct of princesses.

Little is known of Jahanara's most private life. Eventually, however, she was officially reinstated into the court and — most likely because she was smarter and more popular than her sister Raushanara — she was made once again the emperor's confidante. She was accorded by her brother the emperor the title Padishah Begum, "Empress of Princesses." Because of her high position in the court, she was allowed to criticize Aurangzeb where others did not dare. Aurangzeb had become even more strict in pursuit of his religious ideals and had forbidden women to wear tight trousers, gamble, engage in musical entertainment, or many of the other amusements of the court and the harem. Jahanara began an active protest against these restrictions and was somewhat successful. She was less successful, however, in her protests against his ruthless treatment of Hindus. She tried desperately to counsel her brother as he proceeded into what could be described only as a politics of hatred and madness, but it was to no avail. Jahanara died at the age of sixty-seven in the year 1681. She bequeathed her finest gems to a favorite niece, Jani Begum, daughter of her brother Dara.

Life in India
in 1627

Historical Note

The Moghul empire in India began with Timur, who was nicknamed Timur-i-Leng, Timur the lame, because of his lame leg. He is also known as Tamerlane. The term Moghul derives from the word "Mongol," the name of the nomadic people who lived to the north of India. Timur was born in 1336 into a Mongol tribe in central Asia that had been under the rule of the great Ghengis Khan. Timur, despite his lameness, proved to be a brilliant and dazzling leader. In 1398, he led an army across the Indus River, the first natural barrier protecting India, the land then known as Hindustan. He arrived several months later in Delhi, which he captured.

Timur did not choose to stay for long, however. After his great military accomplishment, he returned to his own capital city of Samarkand. With him he took some of India's finest craftsmen, for he was enamored with the art, paintings, cloth, and jewelry that he had found.

The splendor that was India did not escape him, and he was determined to make these arts live in his own country. These high artistic achievements were carried on by the descendants of Timur in the courts of his regions, which are now known as the countries of Afghanistan and Uzbekistan.

Islam was the religion of these newcomers from the north. They were known as Muslims and followed the teachings of their prophet Muhammad, who had been born around the year 570 A.D. Without exception, all Moghul rulers were Muslims. Although there were many laws within the religion of Islam that guided people in their daily lives, the Moghul court often disregarded the law forbidding the drinking of alcohol. Jahanara's grandfather Jahangir in particular had an uncontrollable addiction to alcohol and drugs that proved fatal.

The first Moghul emperor to stay in India was Babur. It is Babur, who reigned for only four years, who is regarded as the founder of the Moghul Dynasty. Born in 1483, he was a Chaghatai Turk, another Mongol tribe in Asia. Searching for an empire to call his own, he, too, was entranced by the dream of India. Sensitive, deeply artistic, but with all the consummate skills of a warrior-king, he first usurped Samarkand from his cousin. Next, he began to consider the empire to the south so long neglected since

Timur had first conquered it. Babur began his invasion and reconquest of India in 1525. Unlike his ancestor Timur, Babur decided to stay. He began to consolidate the vast territories that comprised India. His new capital was established at Agra.

What Babur had found in these territories were the remnants of the old Moghul rulers appointed by Timur. These remnants had endured as independent Muslim kingdoms. But there were also Hindu states commanded by Rajputs, or Hindu warrior-nobles, in the western part of India. Babur's task was to integrate and consolidate these different provinces into a viable political and economic entity. To do this, Babur had to maintain an open mind about questions of religion and ethnic identity. India became a meeting place for the crosscurrents of cultures, though there was always the threat of rebellion in various provinces.

Babur inherited Timur's love for the arts, particularly gardens that flowed with water. He began to design exquisite gardens with ingenious watercourses, fountains, and pools. The art and design of the water garden was one of the most distinctive contributions of the Moghul emperors, and these gardens can still be viewed today in India and Pakistan. Indeed, the Moghul court became recognized as one of extreme advancement in terms of the arts and the sciences. Many stars and constellations were first discovered and studied by astronomers and astrologers of the Moghul courts.

It was, however, the grandson of Babur, Akbar, whose reign from 1556 to 1605 marked the turning point of the Moghul Dynasty. Precocious and of the sharpest wit and intelligence, it has been forever a mystery as to how this greatest of Moghul rulers could have been completely illiterate. But he could not read. Ascending the throne at age thirteen, he initiated reforms that stretched across many aspects of government, from economic matters to public safety, that stabilized his administration. But most important, perhaps, was his embracing of all faiths and his tolerance for all religions. Indeed, many orthodox Muslims were offended by what they saw as his abandonment of the true religion in order to explore Hinduism, Buddhism, and Christianity. For example, as part of his tolerance practice he realized that his best strategy in subjugating the rebellious Rajput leaders was "matrimonial diplomacy." He married many Rajput princesses. His favorite was the Jodh Bai.

Jahangir, Akbar's son who ruled from 1605 to 1627, and the grandfather of Jahanara, ushered in another great period of artistic expression through his passion for architecture, painting, and gardens. The Farah-Baksh, now known as the Shalimar gardens, were first conceived by Jahangir. Jahangir was a powerful yet tragic figure in Moghul history. Intelligent, extraordinarily dedicated to all the arts from architecture to gardens to paintings, many of the very best examples of Moghul arts are directly credited to him. Yet he was plagued by a myriad of addictions, from alcohol to opium. His second wife, Nur Mahal, crafty yet equally intelligent, was a powerful but frightening presence. She became in effect the ruler for the last years of his reign, wielding her power ruthlessly.

Shah Jahan was the son of Jahangir and his first wife, Sher Afghan. He seemed to inherit many good traits from both his father and his grandfather and very little of the bad. He was truly devoted to Mumtaz Mahal, his second wife, but had three other wives, about any of whom little is known. Mumtaz Mahal was truly his first love.

Aurangzeb, the son whom Shah Jahan did not want to rule, became emperor and continued to adhere to Muslim orthodox practices to the point that he eventually outlawed all portrait painting and even forbade the painting and carving of animal figures in decorative work. Austere, puritanical, and utterly ruthless, Aurangzeb imprisoned his father and murdered his brothers. Although other Moghul rulers followed, Aurangzeb was the last of the very powerful ones. The seeds for the decline of the Moghul empire were sowed during his reign from 1658 to 1707, as the non-Muslim populations began to rebel against his harsh decrees and treatment. The Rajputs began to take advantage of the weakening empire and gradually reclaimed the Hindu states that the Moghuls had conquered. In the meantime, there was an expanding European presence in India, in particular a growing British influence. The East India Company, which had started as a trading company, had become a powerful military force by the end of the seventeenth century and began a policy of systematic territorial expansion. The phrase "the sun Never sets on the British empire" was largely due to the company's conquest of India. In 1858, the British crown imposed direct rule over India and appointed a viceroy. In 1877, without ever setting foot on the continent of India, Queen Victoria of England declared herself Empress of India. In 1915, Mohandas Gandhi, known as the Mahatma, or "great soul," began to campaign for passive resistance to British rule.

In 1947, after years of subjugation and exploitation by the British, India gained its freedom at midnight of August 15, and what was known as the British Raj came to an end. Jawalharlal Nehru became India's first independent prime minister. But India was divided at that time into two countries: the primarily Hindu nation of India and the Muslim nation of Pakistan. During this partition there was phenomenal violence between Hindus and Muslims that claimed more than half a million lives. In 1948, a Hindu fanatic assassinated Mahatma Gandhi.

Today, India is the largest democracy in the world. But there is still terrible violence between the Muslims and the Hindus and between India and Pakistan.

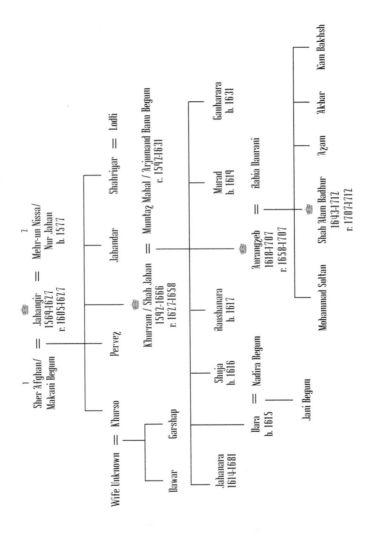

Sher Afghan / Makani Begum =₁ Jahangir 1569-1627 r. 1605-1627 =₂ Mehr-un Nissa / Nur Jahan b. 1577

Wife Unknown = Khurso   Pervez   Khurram / Shah Jahan 1592-1666 r. 1627-1658 = Mumtaz Mahal / Arjumand Banu Begum c. 1592-1631   Jahandar   Shahriyar = Lodli

Dawar   Garshap

Jahanara 1614-1681   Dara b. 1615 = Nadira Begum   Shuja b. 1616   Raushanara b. 1617   Aurangzeb 1618-1707 r. 1658-1707 = Rabia Daurani   Murad b. 1619   Gauharara b. 1631

Jani Begum

Mohammad Sultan   Shah Alam Badhur 1643-1712 r. 1707-1712   Azam   Akbar   Kam Bakhsh

The Moghul Dynasty Family Tree

In the sixteenth century, the Moghul Dynasty had the greatest and most magnificent rulers in India. Great lovers of the arts, they fostered the composition of beautiful poetry, music, and paintings. They commissioned exquisite jewelry and built extraordinary buildings. All the while, these cultured men also engaged in ruthless battles — fathers against sons, brothers against brothers — in their ambitious claims for the throne. The emperor Babur is regarded as the true founder of the incredible dynasty. His son Humayun followed his reign, and, upon his sudden death, his son Akbar rose to power. From him came the emperors Jahangir, and his successor, his son Shah Jahan, the father of Jahanara. Their Moghul Dynasty reigned supreme until its eventual end in 1858 when the British invaded India and rose to power. The family tree chart shows Jahanara's royal lineage beginning with her grandfather. Dates of birth and death (when available) are noted. The crown symbol indicates those who ruled. Double lines represent marriages; single lines indicate parentage.

Jahangir: Jahanara's grandfather; father of Shah Jahan. The eldest son of the great emperor Akbar, Jahangir became king after the death of his father, who reigned for forty-nine years.

Nur Jahan: Jahanara's aunt and step-grandmother. Wife and trusted adviser to Jahangir, she was the sister of Asaf Khan, Jahangir's senior minister and the father of Mumtaz Mahal.

Shah Jahan: Jahanara's father, also named Khurram; the third son of Jahangir. Upon his father's death, and after the death of his three brothers, he became king. He died in 1666 and was entombed with his wife in the Taj Mahal, the magnificent mausoleum he had built for her memorial.

Mumtaz Mahal: Jahanara's mother, also named Arjumand Banu Begum; beloved wife of Shah Jahan and daughter of Asaf Khan. Together she and Shah Jahan had seven surviving children; she suffered seven miscarriages. She died in 1631, giving birth to their fourteenth child.

Children of Shah Jahan and Mumtaz Mahal

Jahanara: Eldest daughter of Shah Jahan and Mumtaz Mahal. A trusted adviser and caregiver to her father, Jahanara nursed him during his illness until his death. She never married, and she died in 1681 at age sixty-seven.

Dara: Jahanara's brother; eldest and favorite son of Shah Jahan and Mumtaz Mahal. He was executed by his brother Aurangzeb in a fight for the throne.

Shuja: Jahanara's brother; second son of Shah Jahan and Mumtaz Mahal. He escaped execution by his brother Aurangzeb. It's unclear how he met his death.

Raushanara: Jahanara's sister; second daughter of Shah Jahan and Mumtaz Mahal. Like Jahanara, she also never married.

Aurangzeb: Jahanara's brother; third son of Shah Jahan and Mumtaz Mahal. He seized the throne from his father and imprisoned him in Agra. He ruled as king until his death in 1707.

Murad: Jahanara's youngest brother, fourth son of Shah Jahan and Mumtaz Mahal. He was also executed by Aurangzeb in a fight for the throne.

Gauharara: Jahanara's youngest sister; last child of Shah Jahan and Mumtaz Mahal.

Although Princess Jahanara is a revered icon in India, pictures of her are extremely rare. This opaque watercolor on paper (circa 1635), A Young Lady Beneath a Tree, *is said to be a portrait of this favorite daughter of Shah Jahan.*

Shah Jahan, one of the greatest of all Moghul rulers, is captured here in this portrait, a miniature on ivory from Persia.

Beloved wife of Shah Jahan, the beautiful Mumtaz Mahal is portrayed in this matching miniature portrait on ivory.

حشریہ حضرت جہانگیر یا ۃ کہ شبیہ حضرت اکبر یا ۃ رامی بینہ

An early seventeenth-century Moghul miniature portrait depicting Shah Jahan's father, Shah Jahangir, holding a portrait of his own father, the great Shah Akbar.

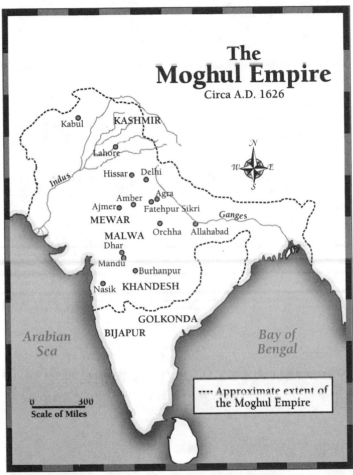

The
Moghul Empire
Circa A.D. 1626

Kabul

KASHMIR

Lahore

Hissar   Delhi

Indus

Amber   Agra

Ajmer   Fatehpur Sikri

MEWAR   *Ganges*

MALWA   Orchha   Allahabad

Dhar

Mandu

Burhanpur

Nasik   **KHANDESH**

GOLKONDA

BIJAPUR

*Arabian
Sea*

*Bay of
Bengal*

0   300
Scale of Miles

---- **Approximate extent of
the Moghul Empire**

*A map of India, circa 1626. The dotted lines indicate the vast area that constituted
the Moghul Empire. Lahore, the birthplace of Shah Jahan, is in modern-day
Pakistan.*

Considered one of the greatest architectural masterpieces in history, the Taj Mahal is the tomb of Shah Jahan's beloved wife, Mumtaz Mahal. The edifice, which is located on the southwestern bank of the Yamuna River in Agra, was constructed entirely of white marble and gold by twenty thousand workmen over the course of twenty-two years.

The Red Fort in Delhi, northern India, was once the imperial home of Shah Jahan and his family. Nine years in the making and completed in 1648, the compound, with impressive buildings made of red sandstone and white marble, is surrounded by a massive 110 foot–high defensive outer wall.

This view from the interior of the Red Fort reflects the exquisite detailing and fine intricacies in design attributed to Moghul architecture.

A seventeenth-century Moghul print of Shah Jahan on his spectacular peacock throne. A symbol of the Shah's elaborate taste and desire for perfection, the throne rests beneath an extensive covering made of silver and gold. It was adorned with precious jewels such as rubies, emeralds, diamonds, and pearls and was surrounded by silk carpets and drapery.

A drawing (above) of the Koh-i-Nor diamond inside a protective cage at the 1851 World's Fair in London. Discovered in the Golconda mines of South India in 1550, the diamond originally weighed about 186 carats. After being passed down through several Moghul and Persian rulers, it was seized by the British in 1848 and placed among Queen Victoria's crown jewels. The queen had the gem reduced to 109 carats and today it is the center stone in the crown on the left (below), which belonged to Queen Mary.

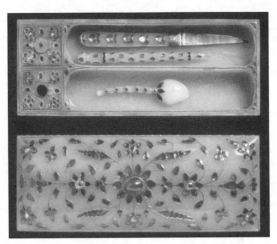

The Moghul Dynasty is celebrated for producing items of elaborate artistry and craftsmanship. This white nephrite jade pen set (above) exemplifies the intricate detail and flamboyant designs of the Moghul era. The box and its contents are embellished with emeralds, diamonds, rubies, and gold. The bird-shaped pendant (below) is encrusted with numerous gemstones and pearls.

Glossary of Indian Words

balashahi: fried pastry

barfi: fudgelike sweetmeat made of milk, sugar, and crushed almonds

Bhagavad Gita or Bhagavadgita [Sanskrit, "The Song of the God"]: eighteen-part dialogue on the meaning of life

bhang: hemp plant of India

Bharata natyam: old classical Indian dance

bindi: dot traditionally worn by Hindu women, between their eyes, as a symbol of marriage

caltrops: spiked instruments, similar to stakes

cholis: blouse

churidaars: women's trousers, tight-fitting from the ankle to the knee

Diwan-i-Am: the Hall of Public Audience

Diwan-i-Khas: the Hall of Private Audience

durbar: public assembly when people and officials bring
their business to the emperor

eunuch: castrated man; formerly such men were employed
as attendants and guards in harems

fakir: literally, "poor man"; specifically, a mendicant
Muslim miracle- or wonder-worker

ghungroos: bells worn by Indian dancers around their
ankles
Ghusl Khana: literally, "bathing room"; also refers to the
most private council chamber of the emperor
gulab jamun (rose sweets): milk dough dumplings in syrup
flavored with rosewater

halwa: sweet candy made of almond paste
howdah: canopied seat with a railing, placed on the back of
an elephant

jalis: perforated stone screen
jama: men's robe
julabmost: fruited ice

kameez: trousers and tunic-like top worn by Indian women

kathak: a dance form from northern India

Koran: Muslim sacred text; the foundation of Islamic religion, law, politics, and culture

kos: unit of measure equal to three miles

Kshatriyas: Hindu upper caste, primarily warriors

Machli Bhawan: fish house

mahout: elephant driver

mandap: canopy used in a Hindu wedding

mudras: hand gestures used in Bharata natyam dance

muezzin: crier who calls Muslims to prayer five times a day from the minaret of a mosque

mullah: teacher of Muslim doctrine

Naqarkhana: drum house and part of the imperial orchestra that accompanied ceremonial processions

nautch dancers: Indian women dancers who often entertained in the Moghul courts

Nawroz: literally, "new day"; the Moghul (originally Persian) New Year, celebrated on the first day of spring (March 21)

nimki: fried dough pastry popular in the Moghul court

paan: betal leaf used in remedies for digestive disorders

pairhan: tunic robe worn by women

palanquin: covered passenger carriage or litter carried by men in India

peshwaz: tunic-like dress of very sheer material worn by Moghul women

puja: Hindu offering to a god

Panch Mahal: five-story pavilion located in the Fatehpur Sikri

purdah: the seclusion of women from the sight of men; a screen or veil was used to insure that the women could not be seen

raita: yogurt with cucumber

Rajput: Hindu warrior-noble of western India

Ramayana: Hindu epic that tells the story of Prince Rama and his wife, Sita

shamiana: colorful canopy used in a garden under which feasts were held

shikara: slender boats

Sufi: follower of a more mystical branch of Islam

sura: section or chapter of the Koran

thali: large platter or tray for serving food

zenana: apartments of a harem

Glossary of Characters

(* indicates fictional character)

FAMILY

Akbar — Jahanara's great-grandfather

*Alafara — Christian concubine of Shah Jahan

Arjumand Banu Begum (Ami) — Jahanara's mother, Empress Mumtaz Mahal

Asaf Khan — Jahanara's maternal grandfather

Aurangzeb — Jahanara's younger brother

Barbur — Jahanara's great-great-great grandfather

Dara — Jahanara's eldest brother

*Indira (Didi) — third wife of Shah Jahan

Jahanara (Janni) — eldest daughter of Shah Jahan

Jahangir — Jahanara's paternal grandfather

*Jaytayu (Jay Jay) — little girl whom Jahanara adopts

Murad — Jahanara's youngest brother

Nur Mahal (The Snake) — wife of Jahangir

Raushanara — Jahanara's younger sister

*Samina — fourth wife of Shah Jahan

Shah Jahan (Aba) — father to Jahanara; Prince
    Khurram; Emperor of the World

Shahrıyar — brother of Aba

Shuja — Jahanara's younger brother

*Swarup — niece of Indira

Tali (The Persian) — first wife of Shah Jahan

ASSOCIATES (SERVANTS, DOCTORS, TUTORS,
ARMY PERSONNEL, ETC.)

Abdul Fazi — astrologer

Abdul-Hamid Lahawri — chronicler of Aba's reign

Abdullah Khan — loyal general

Bhola — court painter

Bulaki — false emperor, the Winter King

*Chitra — servant, "physical therapist"

Commander Wazir Beg — commander of the
    infantry

General Khan Jahan Lodi — once most trusted
    general

*Hamid — blind gardener

*Jumpha — servant

Kareem Sind — imperial steward

Khan Dawran — loyal general

Mirza — wet nurse

Mustafa Azir — chief mullah of the royal court

*Panipat — eunuch

Payag — court painter

Peter Mundy — East India Company representative
   in India

Raja Jujhar Singh Bundela — Deccan rebel

Sati-un Nissa (Satty) — Ami's lady-in-waiting, tutor

Sayidd Jahan Barha — loyal general

Wazir Khan — doctor

About the Author

Kathryn Lasky traveled to India a year and a half before she began writing the Royal Diary of *Jahanara, Princess of Princesses.* When she went to India, Lasky knew very little about Indian culture or history. And she had never heard of the Begum Sahib Jahanara. Lasky said that in the back of her mind she thought she might indeed find a princess on this trip to write about, but she knew so very little that she couldn't imagine where to begin looking.

The author says that the first time she ever heard the name Jahanara was when she was actually standing in the Palace of the Red Fort of Agra in the very rooms of Jahanara. She was captivated by the faded splendor of these apartments. "I heard the guide saying that these were the apartments designed and built especially for Shah Jahan's favorite child, the Begum Sahib Jahanara, and that Jahanara was the child of Shah Jahan and his beloved wife Mumtaz Mahal, for whom the Taj Mahal was built. All my life I had certainly heard of the Taj Mahal, but never had I heard about the daughter of this romantic couple. I remember standing by the carved pool in which Jahanara had bathed and probably swum in. I closed my eyes and tried to imagine what this had looked like when jasper and jade, lapis lazuli and carnelian — all sorts of gemstones — were embedded in the walls around it. I tried to envision the flickering perfume lamps in the niches. To be the favorite daughter of the Emperor of the World and be steeped in jewels, but to have to always live hidden behind the screens of purity, must have been both wonderful and terrible at the same time. I decided I wanted to find out all I could about this Moghul princess and especially what it was like to live in the splendors of the Moghul court at this time."

Of all the Royal Diaries that Lasky has written, this one, she says, has been the most challenging. "I am hardly royal. So I can't claim personal knowledge of royal trappings," she said. "But at least when I was researching the other princesses I have written about, they were Western ones. Their religion, the food, the words, the fashions, were already familiar to me, but when I began to write about Jahanara, I entered a world that was completely foreign and the most exotic environment I had ever heard or seen or read about."

It is important to Lasky that readers understand that, although these are fictional diaries, she has done extensive research so that most of the characters are real and what she knows of their personalities is true. Very little, however, was known of the emperor's three other wives. Indira, the Hindu wife, was a creation of Lasky's for the dramatic purposes of the story. But Lasky did use the diaries of Shah Jahan known as the *Padshahnama*, written by Abdul-Hamid Lahawri. Peter Mundy was indeed a real person who worked for the East India Company, and in his diaries there are several references to the Princess Jahanara. It may be assumed that he did have some kind of contact with her.

Lasky, on one occasion, used what she called some "poetic license." She says that she was truly astonished by the length that the court would go to completely isolate women through their practice of purdah and the screens of purity.

It was indeed recorded in various diaries that when a girl or woman became sick a doctor could only examine the patient by inserting his hands through a curtain and never actually examining the sick person with his eyes. The author imagined that, if this were true, it would possibly be forbidden for a servant to ever touch a princess. For the purposes of the story, Kathryn Lasky included the

detail that it was prohibited for any servant to touch a
royal personage, except for the purposes of such things as
henna decorations and help in dressing.

There is, Kathryn Lasky says, no historical evidence of
the specific non-touching practice, "but I can easily imagine that it might have been."

Lasky says, "From all I could gather, Princess Jahanara
was indeed a young woman of great intelligence and tolerance. If she had been able to rule, I am completely confi-
dent that she would have been in the tradition of her
father and great-grandfather. That, of course, is the fun
part of writing these fictional diaries: I, as a writer, can always imagine 'what if?' So for me the story never really
ends."

Acknowledgments

Cover painting by Tim O'Brien

Page 163 : Portrait of Jahanara, India Office Library and Records, The British Library, London.

Page 164 : Portrait of Shah Jahan, The Granger Collection, New York, New York.

Page 165 : Portrait of Mumtaz Mahal, The Granger Collection, New York, New York.

Page 166 : Portrait of Jahangir with Akbar, Giraudon/Art Resource, New York, New York.

Page 167 : Map of India, courtesy of Scholastic India, Gurgaon, India, re-created by Jim McMahon.

Page 168 (top): Taj Mahal, SuperStock, Jacksonville, Florida.

Page 168 (bottom): Red Fort, SuperStock, Jacksonville, Florida.

Page 169: Interior of Red Fort, Werner Forman Archive/Art Resource, New York, New York.

Page 170: Peacock Throne, Victoria & Albert Museum, London/Art Resource, New York, New York.

Page 171 (top): Koh–i–Nor diamond on exhibit, Bettman/Corbis, New York, New York.

Page 171 (bottom): Koh–i–Nor diamond, Corbis, New York, New York.

Page 172 (top): Moghul pen box, Victoria & Albert Museum, London/Art Resource, New York, New York.

Page 172 (bottom): Moghul pendant, Reúnion des Musées Nationaux/Art Resource, New York, New York.

Other books in The Royal Diaries series

ELIZABETH I
Red Rose of the House of Tudor
by Kathryn Lasky

CLEOPATRA VII
Daughter of the Nile
by Kristiana Gregory

MARIE ANTOINETTE
Princess of Versailles
by Kathryn Lasky

ISABEL
Jewel of Castilla
by Carolyn Meyer

ANASTASIA
The Last Grand Duchess
by Carolyn Meyer

NZINGHA
Warrior Queen of Matamba
by Patricia C. McKissack

KAIULANI
The People's Princess
by Ellen Emerson White

LADY OF CH'IAO KUO
Warrior of the South
by Laurence Yep

VICTORIA
May Blossom of Britannia
by Anna Kirwan

MARY, QUEEN OF SCOTS
Queen Without a Country
by Kathryn Lasky

SŎNDŎK
Princess of the Moon and Stars
by Sheri Holman

ELEANOR
Crown Jewel of Aquitaine
by Kristiana Gregory

Copyright © 2002 by Kathryn Lasky.

Library of Congress Cataloging-in-Publication Data

Lasky, Kathryn.
Jahanara, Princess of Princesses / by Kathryn Lasky.
p. cm. — (The royal diaries)
Summary: Beginning in 1627, Princess Jahanara, first daughter of Shah Jahan
of India's Moghul Dynasty, writes in her diary about political intrigues, weddings,
battles, and other experiences of her life. Includes historical notes on Jahanara's
later life and on the Moghul Empire.
ISBN 0-439-22350-4
1. Jahanara, Begum, 1614–1680 — Childhood and youth — Juvenile fiction.
2. Shah Jahan — Juvenile fiction. 3. India — History — 1526–1765 —
Juvenile fiction. 4. Moghul Empire — Juvenile fiction. [1. Jahanara, Begum,
1614–1680 — Childhood and youth — Fiction. 2. Shah Jahan — Fiction.
3. India — History — 1526–1765 — Fiction. 4. Moghul Empire — Fiction.
5. Princesses — Fiction. 6. Diaries — Fiction.] I. Title. II. Series.
PZ7.L3274 Jah 2002

[Fic] — dc21   2001057627

10 9 8 7 6 5 4 3 2 1   02 03 04 05 06

The display type was done in Solstice.
The text type was set in Augereau.
Book design by Elizabeth B. Parisi

Printed in the U.S.A.   23
First printing, September 2002